To Deborah

SCORCHING STEAM

Love

by

Jillian L Xavier

Dedicated to Lovers

Special Dedication to the love of my life, you thanked me for all I did for you and told me to go publish this book.

Well I did it and I love you very much. You are now my Angel in heaven. At 18yrs old you were gone to soon. Thank you for being the best son a Mother can have. I live my life for you my Angel. D'Andre Jamal Fanniel I'll see you when I get there. You are my biggest Inspiration and you should know that you are always on my mind. Love Mama

Special thanks to everyone that purchase this book enjoy!

Sexy 1

Working late tonight but I can't stop thinking about Sebastian my love making King and my best friend. Last night was so sexy; the things this man does to me! Damn it, I swear my mind is all over the place today even though I can't get last night out of my head I've got to snap out of it and get this financial report in to Mr. Get on my fucking nerves Jordan. see I work at Wise CPA office we handle our client's financials and I need to work because I need Gucci type of money, not to talk about the student loans I should pay back. so, I put up with his demanding and annoying ass.

Came on board two years ago after attaining my Master's Degree in Accounting. It's been a learning experience so far, I'm sure things can be worst! Hmm shaking off my thoughts, the phone buzzed Mya I need those reports right now! I am so tempted to reply I need you to lick the lining of my cunt right now, but I refrain and quickly reply ok Mr. Jordan I will be right in. In retrospect, I should have beaten his ass with temptation making him heel to my every word but damn I was not hypnotize but dicknotize with

Sebastian; come fuck me please sexy ass!

That man drives me so fucking insane I swear between my legs are wet right now come on Mya stay focus I said to myself before walking into the office. Mr. Jordan is feeling me up with his eyes staring at me from head to toe I'm looking at his drooling ass and I'm thinking to myself like if you were the last dick on earth I would fuck myself with a damn tree limb before I let you touch my ass with your Viagra old looking ass. Coming back to reality I said Sir here is the reports you requested! Thank you, Mya let's look here at what we have for this month. After a brief silence Mr. Jordan says well it looks like we made it this month, we have a good report and clients are paying in a timely manner. Did you send out the statements for this month? I did Mr. Jordan I replied. Very well! Mya, we should have lunch in honor of all the hard work says Mr. Jordan.

I said thank you Sir I'll have to take a rain check on this I have a lunch date with my mother and I cannot reschedule. Very well then Mya another time! smh, I know he is looking for a reason to go to lunch, but I cannot be seen in public with his ass. Smiling I said sure another time! Will that be all Sir? Nodding his head, I quickly exit Mr. Jordan office breathing a sigh of relief. Now on to the next one, where was I hmm, oh yes thinking about last night with Sebastian after beating my clit with his tongue ferociously and hungrily, hmm taste me baby I whisper you making me cum like for the twenty forth million-time ok it was four times, but I swear it felt like twenty million my damn legs damn near gave out on me.

I'm thinking to myself feet don't fail me now as Sebastian tells me to stand up and bend over, so he can hit it doggy style! I can hear Snoop saying do it doggy style in my mind shaking the thoughts off while forbidding this damn song to be stuck in my head all night; I quickly focused on the swelling of Sebastian dick close to my ass I said hold up baby you going to need lube for that! Groaning Sebastian says oh baby I am not going there right now I want you where the natural lube is baby! I giggled, but if you want me in your ass Mya I can oblige he says quickly I said oh no you've done enough damage for the night as he eased into me his fingers slide over my clit I push is hands away baby I'm so sensitive after your brutal punishment from your tongue he ignores me massaging my clit with his fingers ooh shit I damn near about to give up the ghost my body is shaking as he slides his hooked dick inside of me.

In and out slowly calling my name breathing in a sexy seductive voice baby this feeling gets more intense every time I love to feel your tight pussy around my dick as he whispers, groaning yes baby I can feel your dick all up in my esophagus with a deep sensual laugh Sebastian says that's right baby that's what a big hook dick do now wet me down with your juices whispering in my ear cum for me sexy.

I immediately obey his command and came screaming oh baby bite my neck and fuck me hard breathing heavily Sebastian starts giving me some daddy long strokes I'm pulling my nipples, feeling his fingers on my clit with his dick in me I cry out oh Daddy I'm about to explode again in a sexy voice Sebastian says come for daddy Mya hearing those words it started to build higher and higher grinding my clit on his fingers he started to go faster and it quicken and I came screaming his name.

For a one moment there I can here I bet the neighbors know my name blasting in my head shaking that out of my mind hmm I swear I'm like a fucking juke box. Sebastian seems to be going for the gold as he slaps my ass groaning loud in my ear I'm about to explode I arch my ass, so his dick has free access to my pussy, pumping harder Sebastian growls I'm about to cum in this pussy baby.

I'm thinking Oh shit talk nasty to me cause I'm about to cum too I said get it baby that's your pussy with those words he exploded trembling we both fell on the bed holding each other his sexy ass with the bald head that I love and my chocolate mocha skin on his caramel skin makes me want to suck his dick, but my ass can't move I've been officially put to bed.

Coming back to reality oh shit I'm in my office drawers wet and shit I'm going to need my (BOB) Battery operated boyfriend I think I got my bullet in my purse off to the restroom I'll have to use the handicap one because it's a single stall and I will be in there alone. Trying to sneak out quickly I clock out for lunch passing Mr. Jordan office he yells out have a good lunch Mya oh don't worry I will nosey bastard, rolling my eyes I responded thank you Mr. Jordan.

That's my representative talking she is my conscious or should I say my bitch she keeps me quiet I love her sometimes. Off to the bathroom it's not available damn I hope nobody not- funk'n up the bathroom. I could go in the broom closet and lock the door, shit I need to get off people shit as soon as I thought about it!

The door open and to my surprise it was the cleaning lady oh thank you I was not trying to pass the fuck out from any funk that will indeed kill the mood I say hi to the lady and as I entered the bathroom after locking the door I searched for my Battery- Operated Boyfriend then I called Sebastian he answers on the first ring what's up baby he said I said just thinking about last night he said Oh!

And... and I'm about to make myself cum I thought you would like to hear me? Are you at work? I am at work I said I am in a single bathroom in mind I'm like shut the fuck up before you ruin this for me sensing my frustration over the phone he says ok let me hear you baby, standing with my back against the wall placing one foot on the sink I slide my panties to the side damn I'm so fucking wet I said he groans I start the toys and zoom I started panting trying not to slump over into the sink due to my legs shaking he said baby you making my dick hard it didn't take long within seconds I came panting trying to stifle a loud groan Sebastian is panting too shit baby go home now I will meet you there take an extended lunch I don't give a fuck call in sick for the rest of the day because my dick is on six o clock and I need to fuck you hard.

Ok I said quickly let me tidy up see you at home looking at myself in the mirror my conscious was like bitch you is nasty dismissing my thoughts I pull the Summers Eve wipes out of my purse and cleaned up the best way I could. Catching my breath and changing my demeanor I called Mr. Jordan he answers hello I said hello in my so fucking sick voice I said sir I ate tuna and my stomach is in knots I need to go home for the rest of the day sounding pitiful as fuck. he said Mya please go take care of yourself I told you about eating from the deli they are not sanitary at all.

Even though my mind was saying shut the fuck up, my bitch was like calm down Mya, so I said I know Mr. Jordan thank you I will see you tomorrow everything on my desk is up to date with that he said fine hope you feel better and hung up. Giving the hand motion with a big yes I left for home through the lobby pressing the elevator frantically like please come on as the door opened, I fixed my face to seem as if I'm hurting just in case Mr. Jordan was in the elevator I knew he had an eleven thirty with the CEO Mr. Wise fine but married ass as the door open I saw Gisele her green eyes piercing with a big smile and sigh of relief I said hi

Gisele how are you she blushed oh I am fine Mya and you looking good and smelling good as always grinning I said yes thanks to Ralph Lauren Glamorous honey which is so hard to find these days. I looked at her so you're heading to lunch she said yes would you like to join me? Looking at Gisele I said I would love too but I ate some tuna which is making my stomach growl, so I am heading home for the day. Disappointed she said ok well, hope you feel better Mya.

I said thank you in my mind I'm thinking if I did not know better I would think this bitch is trying to make a pass at me I would let her eat it if she tried. My conscious screams in my head to get a fucking grip as the elevator open to the first floor, Gisele and I walk side to side I said okay Gisele see you later and she said later babes! I scowl at my mind see I told you that hefer wanted some staying focus at the task at hand I know Sebastian is waiting on me I flag a cab jumping in Gisele got back in my head maybe my ass is on fire and misreading her expressions still wondering if Sebastian would like to watch her assault my-his pussy hmm.

Ok shit let me focus I said to the driver head towards the

Galleria please I'll tell you what street to turn on. And that's only because I cannot remember what street I live on I know it when I see my mind is all over the place today apologizing to the cab driver who quickly said no problem ma'am. I am so confused right now but I better get my shit together before I see Sebastian, as the cab is closer I said take a left at the next stop light then a quick right ok right here thank you I paid the fare and exit quickly running upstairs fumbling for my keys Sebastian open the door stark naked with his dick in his hand he knows that turns me on I pushed pass him stripping my clothes now in my cum fuck me pumps.

I said you ready for me baby even though he said his dick was at six o clock it, look more like twelve o clock from where I stand, and my insides are creaming right now! Getting down on my knees I summoned Sebastian closer stroking his dick he walks slowly towards me he knows it turns me red when I see him massage his dick I'm about to combust without even being touched as he moved closer, he says what exactly are you going to do to me tell me? I giggle Oh Daddy I can show you better than I can tell you sticking my tongue out Sebastian slaps his dick on my tongue opening my mouth I am, looking- into his eyes as he sticks his dick in my mouth. I lick each side sucking slowly as my tongue circling around the tip as I go up and down on his shaft sucking and licking all in one motion.

Sebastian, cries out Oh baby you suck me off so good, yep you damn right who is your bitch thinking to myself then he says suck my dick hard baby I want to cum in your mouth and I oblige going up and down sucking with love wanting to taste him as the pre- cum hits my tongue I placed my hand on his balls massaging them gently Sebastian pushes his head back massaging his balls in my hand simultaneously sucking going up and down on his shaft, I go under and start licking his balls while jacking him off I go up to his dick suck then go to his balls unable to handle the pressure as he knees quake. He grabs my head pulling me in as he grind, his dick in my mouth pulling my head back and forth loving to please him I deep throat his dick screaming out my name he cum I damn near choke but big girls don't cry so I swallow all of him as if it was baileys cream going down my throat with a shot of fuck portion still licking as he holds my head steady.

I swallow all of him, Oh! baby he said lifting me from my knees we head to the bedroom I know I just broke his ass down and the look on my face says I got yah! Laying on the bed Sebastian whispers in my ear so tell me what were you thinking about at work that make you want to get yourself off without me baby? I said the assault you did with your tongue had me reminiscing. Sebastian responds Oh is that right! Well after the payback you put on me this evening I've got to take this to another level where is your toy I close my legs tight saying it's in my Gucci purse he reaches for my bag finding my bullet I squeeze my legs again.

Oh! now Mya open them legs for me now he demanded as if I had a remote between them legs I open them wide on his command okay here we go he says I want you to watch everything I want your eyes on me at all times Mya, Understood. Breathing softly, I said yes. Good! Sebastian started kissing my forehead down to my nose my lips my tongue. Kissing me lovingly we were telling each other how much we're in love without a word I'm breathing heavily and so is he, moving down to my left nipple ripe as it is he can make me come like this sucking and pulling making me squirm sucking the right nipple I can feel in all the way down south with his fingers exploring my sex I want to cum but he torture me by stopping!

He kisses my navel reaching my clit he sucks with delicious pleasure you would swear it was finger licking good grinding to his movement Sebastian holds me still putting the toy on and with anticipation he seduces my body holding the toy in his hand he passes it up and down my clit inside me as he licks he sticks the bullet in me as it vibrates with Sebastian licking my clit I cum hard and screaming sitting up in the bed as my body convulsed cries as I yell his name out loud.

Ready for this dick sexy? yes, I reply and before I can think he pulls me over so I'm sitting on his dick in my mind I am thinking oh shit I can't move pulling me in Sebastian pushes me up and down suddenly. I forgot I was tired as the fire start burning inside moving seductively craving every stroke I started to build up an orgasm moving up and down and round and around being in full motion sucking his tongue I cum again and again. So much for a fake stomach ache I said oh that's how you got out of work today?

Yep the culprit name is tuna laughing I got up hit the showers and then off to make dinner for my man while I am in the shower my mind ran on the elevator meeting with Gisele damn her ass is fine too as I dream about her kissing me all over while Sebastian watched I got hot again hmm. Stop my conscious nags me to stop it so I hurry out the shower thinking what to cook I decided to curry some chicken with potatoes beginning to cook I can hear Sebastian singing in Spanish sounds so sweet all I can make out is mi amour he is my everything I can't stay mad at him for a long time when he flashes that smile I just melt away. Dinner is ready honey! Sebastian yells let's eat in the living room babe the basketball game is on.

That's cool honey so I place our plates on a tray and off to watch the game with my baby we try not to bring work home so it's usually one liner. How was work I said he waves one hand fine and you he says I reply fine as we eat he comments on the game I listen intently agreeing to everything he says because right now it's all about him. After putting up the plates with a kiss I whisper baby I'm going to go lay down I think you wore me out. Ok Mya says Sebastian I will be there soon, walking into the bedroom I just wanted to lay down as soon as I hit the sheets I fell asleep.

Dreaming of Gisele touching me sucking my nipple, going down south sticking her tongue in an out of my cunt slowly licking my clit and I'm fondling her breast with my legs open wide as I sit up on the bed looking at her tongue I'm about to cum on this sexy bitch lips I'm right there Oh! Gisele lick that clit baby then footsteps Oh shit, the door slammed Sebastian walks in son of A Bitch I'm horrified oh shit I screamed Cumin and about to pass the fuck out at the same time. Sebastian screams my name Mya wake up shaking me aggressively come on Mya wake up as I wake up I blink twice trying to see clearly Sebastian is leaning over me baby what's wrong? He said did you have a bad dream squeezing my legs I quickly said yes wondering shit I hope I did not talk in my sleep holding me in his arms I snuggle back to sleep barely my mind going crazy with my heart pounding in my chest I am wondering did he hear me? Did I call her name out loud? scolding myself I've got to get my damn hormones in check. Showering for work this morning and thinking back on last night I know I'm over board I quickly get dress gave Sebastian a kiss saying see you later honey and walked out the door. He reacted in his normal way saying keep it wet for me sexy I giggle and head on to work.

As soon as I got in the elevator Gisele says hold the door please oh shit I'm thinking what the hell is my mind playing tricks on me she gets in I said good morning, quietly she said good morning Mya look like you have seen a ghost in the back of my mind I was like if you stay out my fucking dreams you pretty bitch I won't be looking like I'm about to give up the ghost right now. I smiled at her saying Oh no I just had little sleep just a little tired I said, coming close Gisele says so are you feeling better Mya? I was like what huh! Oh, yeah as my mind quickly adjust the tuna thing yes, I feel much better thank you for asking. Good to know Gisele says as the elevator stops on my floor I whisper have a good day to her.

Looking at me intently she blushes saying you do the same. Walking fast, I could not wait for the damn elevator door to close because I can feel her watching my ass as I walked looking back quickly with an awkward wave I catch her licking her lips oh shit my pussy trying to jump out my thongs and run back to the elevator snatching that bitch back by her pubic hairs I put her ass back in my panties.

This is crazy I am doing too damn much! Damn control yourself my conscious warns. Heading in the office Mr. Jordan says Mya how are you feeling while passing his office I said better thank you for asking in my mind I'm like if only you knew shit sex at home is crazy a sexy bitch licking her lips at me I mean the whole shit crazy.

Are there anything critical on the schedule today Sir? I asked. Well I must meet with Mr. Wise again briefly can you organize The Tanner file he wants to look at the PNL ok? I pull the profit and loss statement and placed it on Mr. Jordan desk glancing at me Mr. Jordan asked again if I'm alright? Thinking to myself, mind your damn business old man.

Sexy 2

I replied yes sure wandering if the fluster is showing on my face but being the opportunist that I am I throw in oh you know I am still trying to fight my stomach pain from the tuna yesterday. Mr. Jordan says well if you can finish your entire task quickly you can use your sick time that's what it's for Mya if you need to leave now let me know. Oh no Mr. Jordan I will try to make it if it gets worst I will let you know. Very well, Mya says Mr. Jordan please don't stay on my behalf we are through month end, so this is the best time to be sick smirking he said.

Rolling my eyes in the back of my fucking head thinking like what the fuck ever give me a window of opportunity and let me show you how quick I can jump through that bitch. Thank you again Mr. Jordan I replied is that all Sir? Nodding his head, I step out of Mr. Jordan office I decided to take a quick rest room break standing by the sink looking at myself in the mirror Gisele walks in how fucking convenient I get myself together quickly heading towards the door Gisele says you don't have to leave on my behalf.

I am thinking oh yes bitch I do if I don't I would be in some uncompromising position with your ass, I said oh no I must prep a meeting for my boss catch you later running out the bathroom like a punk I can hear her say ok catch you later Mya! Hmm yeah only with your tongue sexy I whispered. My conscious screamed for real like you really need to stop this shit before you get ahead of yourself. Back in the office I called Sebastian hey babes he says what's up I miss you already honey I said smiling.

Sebastian says don't forget we are meeting Lisa and Josh later so don't be late. I absolutely forgot ok I will be on time it's down time at work now. Kisses baby Sebastian saying see you later responding I said right back at you baby! Hanging up thinking about what am I going to wear tonight even though it casual, its couple date night tonight I've got to look hot for my man. The phone rings its Diamond my sister hey sis what's up? I say nothing what's going on well you know your nieces Mariah birthday is on Saturday. and we are going to Chuck E Cheese so you must come.

Girl I swear if it was not for my niece I would not be caught alive or halfway dead in that damn place so what time is it supposed to be? Two o clock and yeah bring that sexy boyfriend of yours! Good luck with that shit Sebastian isn't gonna come, she sighs but I will ask him ok so see you on Saturday I've got to get back to work.

Later sis she says and I say later and hang up. The day wrapped up quickly off to see Lisa and Josh they are so cute together Lisa is Sebastian baby sister he does these date nights really to keep an eye on Lisa since their father abused his mom he is super sensitive about his sisters and he has a right to. When I arrived home, no one was home so I took the time to sit down and relax my mind; I decided to have a glass of wine since we were not meeting with Lisa and Josh for another hour and my man is not home yet so might as well. I sigh loudly when I think about Chuck E Cheese I really don't want to go but I can't be an ass so I have to go hmm sipping on my wine the door unlocks I jumped up to hug my baby as he comes in the door, happy to see me he says I kissed him let me show you how much kissing his deeply our tongues hungry for each other Sebastian pushing me away slowly, he put his hand on my face and said Mya baby we have to go and I said sure! Taking a quick shower, we got dressed and headed to a Caribbean restaurant they have the best curry chicken, stew fish and the best sugar cake you ever had.

19

It's a Trinidad and Tobago restaurant Auntie Jillian's is what's it's called but everybody calls her Tanti Jilly I guess it's a Trini thing. Sebastian called Lisa to see how far she and Josh were sounding impatient on the phone Sebastian tells her to hurry up. I'm sensing something is wrong is it the dream last night did I say something in a daze Sebastian tugs my arm come on Mya what are you waiting on he says. I shake off my thoughts and smile a half of smile but looking at him intently trying to catch a sign of what's eating him? Or rather what ate me is the question I jumped when the waiter asked if we would be dining in or taking out?

Sebastian answered we will be dining in it's a party of four as we are ushered to our table Lisa and Josh shows up greeting us with a smile and hugs Sebastian looked Lisa over as if he was looking for some sign of abuse Lisa shrugs him off saying really bro are you serious? Mira am look Josh loves me and I love him ain't none of that shit going on over here Sebastian smirked and better yet big brother I can handle myself very well thank you so back off. Hello Mya, how are you doing?

I gave her a tight squeeze whispering I am doing very well; Sebastian smiled and greets Josh with a hand shake that could have bought him to his knees. Waving hello to Josh I quickly said honey smiling, to ease the tension what are you having tonight while looking at the menu, looking at me he says let's get something to drink first ok beers then he ignored me and motion for the waiter.

To come over while he asked him for four Caribs which is a Trinidadian beer I was thinking maybe he needs somewhat crawl up your ass and died drink. Turning my attention to Lisa I asked how was her day and what had she been up to? Lisa started talking about her job telling me that they have a new boss who is currently pissing her off to the fucking extreme. He constantly hits on me Lisa says, I glanced at Sebastian even though he was engaged in a conversation with Josh about the basketball playoffs. He turned to Lisa asking what did you say and Lisa realizing Sebastian had steam coming out his ears with his eyes turning dark. She calmly said bro I can handle myself I'm just filling Mya in on my day!

Ignoring her response Sebastian says so your new boss has eyes for you huh? Turning to Josh in a hurry Sebastian says you better be protecting my sister Josh agreed saying I go every day at lunch to let her new boss know that I am her man the minute he steps out of line it's on bro trust me I got the fucker. Relaxed, Sebastian says cool if you need me let me know! The waiter interrupts asking if we were ready to order Lisa says yes I am starving plus that curry smells delicious, Lisa ordered the curry shrimp dinner with extra plantains, Josh had the stew oxtails dinner, I ordered the stew fish with dumplings and provisions extra sauce on the fish please I requested, Sebastian hmm ok I think I will have the red snapper dinner and oh yeah bring extra plantains for me and another round of Carib for the ladies and two Guinness Stout for us with a hand gesture he looks directly at Josh who agreed. Not like he had a choice the waiter took down our orders and promises it will be right out.

And can you bring some pepper sauce for food, sure the waiter said. Bringing the beers, we toasted to another day that we all are alive and well as our glass clicked with the guy's bottles we drink up. I slip my hand under the table and squeeze Sebastian legs oh Mya he says I'm happy you are here with me don't ever leave me. Taken aback, I reassured him I would never leave. I love you baby where is this coming from? Here goes my conscious bitch you are fucking know should I remind you of the wet dream you had last night. Scowling at my thoughts I concentrate on Sebastian I pulled his face close to mine saying baby I am not going anywhere I promise you that what will make you think otherwise I asked. Sebastian shrug we will talk about it later feeling awkward I looked up and the waiter came with the food. Thank you Lord wow right on time.

Still feeling like, damn I really fucked up now but this is what I need to stay focused one dumb ass mistake courtesy of my fucking hormones can make me lose my man, my life and my all. I told your ass stop why you were ahead my conscious says, shut up I quickly scowl in my mind. Then I started to think sitting on the table if these fools only knew what was going on in my head they would throw my ass in St Ann's. the crazy ward any sane human would think I was mentally unstable, but I don't hear voices though laughing to myself, ok let me rephrase that ok I do hear voices but it's my conscious also known as my bitch two names referenced but one voice. Ok I am laughing loud inside desperately trying to hold back a smile because that will really make me look crazy. Here come my thoughts oh but you are crazy!

Shut the fuck up! As I dismiss that thought in my mind. We

continue to eat, Josh quickly says he got the bill feeling full and satisfied Sebastian says taunting hell yeah you got it bro because I've been handling up every time laughing the bill got paid saying our goodbyes we left for home anxious to get home and talk to Sebastian my nerves started to get bad in retrospect I wondered where did the insecurity come from even though I had a clue I was going to play dumb all the way shit I may be crazy but I am not stupid. Driving home. I decided to lighten the moment, so babe how did your day go today? Oh! just fine he responded and by you placing your hands-on dick oh yeah things just got better. Now that we are alone together smiling Sebastian says it will get even be better when I get home now that the Guinness Stout is doing a number on my dick!

Seizing the opportunity, I started to move my hand to get a feel of his concerns. Oh, damn baby your dick is rock hard let me see if I can alleviate some of that stress. unzipping his pants before he makes it to the stop light I lay my head in his lap releasing the bulge. Taking it all in my mouth he keep saying stop but he's not actually pushing me off his lap, with his two hands on the steering wheel my lips moved up and down on his shaft licking the tip as I come up going down licking the sides over and over, again. Mya, he says please baby let's make it home with a stifle groan I said no, Mya you gonna make me pull over with a hand gesture I said ok keeping a steady pace I can feel him getting rock hard moving my hands up and down as I suck Sebastian says fuck NO!

Very seductively no hands baby let feel the wetness of your mouth and you tongue caressing my dick I'm enjoying this go slow. Giving my man what he wants how he wants it; I place my hands on his thighs as I suck his dick telling him without words I love him and I would never leave him the car stops. I'm groaning to the rhythm of his breathing the car pulls into park groaning hard screaming my name, suck it baby as he reclines his seat giving my mouth more access grinding his dick in my mouth I keep sucking but in my mind. I'm like hurry the fuck up my damn neck hurt shit the reason you holding back is what? Don't make me stop I love you so hurry up and cum before I reintroduce myself and here it goes the blasted rap in my head. My name is oh no… stop shit moving on quickly I got more aggressive on his dick digging for the gold ignoring his plea to slow down please baby I bust that water pipe outing that fire. Sucking him all up with a biscuit not leaving a drip Sebastian trembling Cumin holding my head down Sebastian explodes.

Giving a high five to myself internally I suck him until he is limp like cold pool water hitting his dick hmm limp is the word. Raising my head in triumph I've won the gold now bow to the Queen bitches my conscious was like I wish I would bow to your crazy ass dismissing my thoughts I look at my baby he is sitting in the driver's seat like a wounded dog looking up at the car ceiling. I told my baby I will drive the rest of the way home zipping his pants up he said no I got it as he starts the ignition we head home only a couple of blocks I said so baby was it good to you? Oh! YES, with passion Sebastian whispered come on I got something for you Mya excited and scared as shit I murmur ok baby. We get in the house and it feels good to be home walking to the bedroom I kick off my shoes I started to get undressed Sebastian said stop I will do that throwing my hands up in the air I said ok have it your way baby coming towards me my heart started to beat if there was anything in question he would know so.

I need to calm the fuck down because right now I'm acting guilty when I have not done anything well maybe in my mind and my dream but that does not count does it? As he got closer he unbuttoned my pants and pull the zip down looking at me he says so tell me about the dream you had last night my heart started to pound at that time oh shit I cannot breathe I feel flushed my head started to spin quickly I said what? Sebastian said don't play with me what the fuck were you dreaming last night and be honest! Ok I dreamed that Gisele ah and once the name came out my mouth my conscious was like this is when you needed to lie dumb ass. Urging me to go on I said baby she has a crush on me and yesterday.

When I was on my home to you she was in the elevator asking me to go to lunch when I declined she seam very disappointed it was a weird feeling she kept staring at me. Taking off my shirt he says okay and the dream well I dreamt she was licking me between my legs I breathe looking for a reaction from him he says lift one leg so I can get your pants off then he tap my other leg looking at Sebastian he pulled me down to the bed so in the dream did you touch her he asked I said yes quietly and swallowed hard, tell me how he says while taking my panties off and I'm in to damn deep now so I can't lie to him now sticking his finger inside of me he says Mya you are soaking wet wow so tell me I want to know. I said I was sitting up in the bed she was laying between my legs tasting me and my hands were fondling her breast.

So, touch your breast show me how you did it baby I started to touch them and he sunk his face in between my legs looking at me he said did she licked you like this? Thinking to myself I'm scared to answer that one answer me he says I said something like that but not as good as you do. That's not what I asked you Mya keep touching your tits I like that! With that said started his punishment sucking, licking while sticking his tongue in me I moaned baby all I want is you! And of course, the song "All I want is you" by Miguel started playing in my head. Can somebody cut the fucking juke box off please? I screamed in my head bringing me back to reality Sebastian whispers Mya I know now come for me licking the tip of my clit over and over I came gripping my nipples. They were so hard kissing my inner thighs he slides up on me his dick, hard as a rock sliding inside of me Sebastian says that was some dream you had baby but let me make on fucking thing clear make sure it ends there in a stern voice.

Quietly I said ok baby my conscious was like I told your ass you were doing too much shaking off the thought I reached up to kiss him, so she likes you huh? While he fucks me hard as if to say by the time I damage this pussy she won't want to touch you. Continuing to tease me he said is she pretty he asked hey I thought you said it ends there well giving me more information is ok I'm talking about anything physical. Smiling I said yes, she is pretty teasing I said maybe you should meet her hmm maybe I should meet the woman who wants to claim my pussy we both bust out laughing. Stay quiet he warned pounding hard with his hand on my ass.

Pulling me into his dick I murmur give me all of that hard dick I want to cum on it Oh fuck he says damn cum for me dark and lovely with your sexy ass I need to feel the heat of your cum on my dick while whispering in my ear I am the only one that eats this pussy you understand me ain't no bitch stealing my lunch, I do the fucking dishes.

Smiling I said I agree baby tightening, releasing my cunt around his dick as Sebastian fuck me hard I whisper baby I'm about to cum on your dick. Cum for me baby grinding my hips I came, and he followed calling my name out loud. He slumped on me I hold him tight I will never leave you baby I promise, promise, and promise, promise you babe.

And like a juke box I can hear Jagged Edge song this time I let the record play in my head, we head to the shower together I washed him he washed me feeling satisfied and thoroughly fucked we dried up and head to bed before dozing off I turned to him and said baby I am so happy I can tell you everything I was so damn scared you would be angry because in the dream you came in and slammed the door once you saw us and that's when I screamed then you were waking me up.

Oh! so that explains the reason you were screaming so did she make you cum? That's it baby, this discussion is over I am going to sleep, oh no you don't he says answer my question rolling my eyes I said yes when you came in the door I was Cumming and screaming at the same time with a wicked look on his face he said shit you should have ride my dick last night after that dream I bet you were wet as fuck. Pushing him away I said whatever Sebastian I was too damn scared and worried you heard me talking in my sleep. Well at any rate he says I'm relieved it was a woman and not a man so arrange lunch tomorrow I want to meet Gisele my face hit the floor my mouth was wide open.

Looking at Sebastian he said pick you face from off the floor baby it's obvious you were thinking about letting her touch you and that's why you had that dream, so I want to meet my competition. Picking my face from off the cold ass floor I told him look I don't want her you are it for me I just think my hormones are crazy right now. Yeah, it's crazy alright my conscious scowl! Your dismissed bitch go, the fuck away shaking my head so I can get these damn thoughts out of my head I threw my hands up and say fine consider it done I will arrange lunch. I am going to bed this time I rolled over and held him as he slept blanketing him baby I love you I whisper and kiss his neck feeling him relax I almost want to cry I never felt like I deserved to be love I was such a wayward child growing up.

My parents had no faith in me not that I gave them any reason to in retrospect I've made a lot of bad decisions but looking at me now and how far I've come and finding the love of my life I feel pretty humbled right now as sleep plagued me in silent prayer I begged oh Lord please don't let me dream you know who again I'm scared to call her name because it might stay in my subconscious then the dreams will come so in a mad chant I keep saying Sebastian, Sebastian, Sebastian in my head till I fell asleep. Thank God It's Friday, yes thank you Lord I open my eyes and looked at my baby sleeping so peacefully gently moving my hands from around his waist I ease out of the bed slowly as to not disturb him then he rolls over. Good morning beautiful I say right back at you my love Sebastian says straddling him I kissed his neck thanks for last night I whispered grabbing my ass he says no problem baby.

Now get up you have an assignment today oh yeah, I frowned a lunch arrangement slapping my ass as I get up so make it happen. Ok I said where do you want to meet I asked let's go to Lisa's Deli around the corner from work. Sure, babe I will talk with her she may not be available at all look sexy today she will come but what if I am wrong well we will find that out today go bathe it's getting late. I waived my hand at him hopping in the shower. I can hear my mind loud and clear that's what your ass get go figure shaking my head I dismissed my thoughts like fall back bitch, I don't want to hear it. I get dressed quickly and said see you later to Sebastian who was on the phone with his boss I motioned see you at lunch honey.

I get to work and brace myself as I walked in the building heading to the elevator I spot Gisele waiting for the elevator to come I politely said good morning with a big beautiful smile she replied and a lovely morning it is Mya I get to see you before I get to my office giving her a nervous smile I asked her out to lunch she said sure about twelve will do, I said sure we go on the elevator and Gisele stood in front of me facing me she says you look sexy today Mya are you going to hang out after work I said no I just feel good today.Mya yes Gisele you know I've been thinking about you! Is that right? I said thinking to myself what the fuck this bitch is bold then Gisele did the unthinkable she stopped the elevator stunned I look at her my heart started to jump out my chest fuck my pussy she already left and at attention on Gisele lips waiting to get manipulated with her tongue. I, tried to snatch my pussy back, but that stubborn cunt won't go back in my thong. It's like a candy in a candy store come eat me please! I looked at her and said why did you stop the elevator anything we must discuss we can do it at lunch I have a meeting with my boss coming closer I can feel her heat Gisele whisper in my ear without touching me I want you to sit on my face, I want to taste you.

My pussy was jumping off the fucking hinges I gasp and step back, but I had nowhere to go she had me cornered I can hear Sebastian voice saying no bitch is going to steal my lunch at that point I could not even talk I was helpless my nipples got hard and I can feel extreme heat and warmth between my legs. Finally, I murmured, let's talk at lunch. She smelled like Dolce and Gabbana Rose I know because I wear the same perfume.

She said ok but I want to taste your tongue can I kiss you I looked at her this beautiful female is turning my ass out before I can say a word her soft lips were on mine as she slid her tongue in my mouth her eyes and mines we locked she kissed me and I let her then she closed her eyes as if I had made her dream come through breathing softly she slid her hand around my waist pulling me closer and I kept my hands by my side I was shocked and confused it seems like minutes were going pass when she stopped I stared at her damn you're a great kisser smiling she said thank you. I've never kissed a girl in my life I said I have a boyfriend Gisele please start the elevator this is crazy.

Sexy 3

Touching my face she says I won't interfere with your relationship I just want to taste you when you release your juices, you know when you cum. my body went limp in the back of my mind I wanted her to taste me right now but my inner bitch was pacing the floor so I said we will chat at lunch she started the elevator and it was a dead silence I just wanted to get to my floor Gisele stood to the side of me with her hands in the small if my back I did not move when it came to my floor I said see you at lunch! OH, looking forward to it she said in a very sexy voice her eyes looked misty oh fuck Sebastian going to commit murder on my ass walking out the elevator I knew she was watching my ass but my damn legs were like planks I could not move fast.

I say good morning to Mr. Jordan and went to my desk once I clocked in I got on the phone and called Sebastian when he answered I said ok we are on for lunch, but she thinks it's just her and I so act like you were in the neighborhood. I don't want it to seem like it was planned then Sebastian said so you want me to play coy with my woman hell no he says, come on baby she would not come if I told her I was meeting you and I just want to get this shit over with I feel overwhelmed right now. Why are you overwhelmed he asks because I really don't want to do this so do please see you at noon I have a meeting with my boss now. I hung up the phone exasperated I can hear Katy Perry I kissed a girl and I liked it OH fuck would somebody cut the fucking music off in my head please! I scowl at my mind shut the fuck up! My phone buzz I switch gears quickly answering yes Sir are you ready for the meeting? I will have to reschedule Mya I have a doctor's appointment my wife just called to remind me I will be back later in the day. Ok great! My mind was relieved I will work on the financial statements in the meantime, very well Mr. Jordan say I will call if I can't make it back! Sure Sir thank you. Hanging up the phone breathing a sigh of relief when I heard Mr. Jordan shut his door and walk down the hallway. I immediately shut my door I got the statements and put it in front my computer as to create a facade just in case anybody come in settling down on my chair I pushed back rocking back and forth what have I done oh shit how can I fix this well at least I did not have sex with her it was just a kiss a sweet sexy slow kiss. My conscious was like you in too deep the gospel according to Damian Marley.

I pull out my phone and played the song "In to Deep". I love this cd and the one album he did with NAS who happen to be my favorite rapper I bought his album the first week it drops. Trying to distract myself from the dilemma at hand I play "Dispear" from the Damian and NAS album with my head set on.

I am jamming relaxing myself I let the music take me away from this horny female and my jealous man who is going to cut my ass up as fine as cat shit if he finds out what the fuck happened in the elevator struggling to chase the thoughts out of my mind I tune back into the music looking for a remedy before I know it its time eleven forty five time for lunch cursing in my mind I change the song on my phone I clicked on "Heaven" NAS song of the Godson album the songs comes on " if heaven was a mile away will I pack up my bag and leave this world behind" wow I dig deep into the music I want go home I want to not be at lunch I don't want to play this game and I don't want to see her. I need to find another job this shit ain't gonna work, I love my man I want to scream for help, but nobody is coming except my inner crazy truthful conscious.

Gathering my strength, I head to the lobby it seemed as if this bitch had the elevator on pause because as I walk out I can see her standing there waving at me oh shit here we go I step in thinking to myself you in for a rude awakening worried that things would get ugly hoping the kiss incident don't come up nervously I said hello to Gisele before she could respond I said do not stop the elevator or this lunch is off gazing at me she must of sense some change in my demeanor. So how was your meeting Gisele asked I said he cancelled, keeping my answer short we got to the first floor and I breathe a sigh of relief we made it without any incident my heart started to race as we walk to the deli we arrived and sat down as soon as we did I hear hey babes.

I look around and Sebastian and two of his co-workers Andrew and Ricardo were eating come join us he says feeling like I could make it through the lunch I turn to Gisele and said that's my boyfriend she said ok keeping her composure even though I knew she was disappointed I walked over and give Sebastian a hug and a kiss his boys started teasing get a damn room laughing turned to Gisele and said this is my man Sebastian while still holding on tight to him he shook her and then introduced her to his boys we sat down and ordered sandwiches. Ricardo seem to have the hots for Gisele scooting closer to her he asked her where she from. I leaned towards Sebastian and whispered thank so much for making this less stressful.

I love you he says, and I don't want you to feel overwhelmed about anything. I love you more I said so what do you think about Gisele I asked. Well she is a pretty girl I might let her come over to taste you I'll have to be there to supervise though, my eyes were wide open after processing his words in my head I quickly said you're joking right? Eat your lunch baby I'm just teasing you, then he asked Gisele, so you work with Mya? Gisele said no we work in the same building on different floors. Andrew and Ricardo excuse themselves to use the restroom I am in the middle of Gisele and Sebastian. OH, shit here we go so what do want to do with my girlfriend? Do you have a crush on her? Taken aback Gisele said I do like her but I won't disrespect. What you have, obviously have, I can tell she really loves you. Sebastian responded, and I love her I don't feel uncomfortable with you and her talking but anything else talk to me about it first understood and Gisele said yes.

I jumped in we only have fifteen minutes left we better eat up Andrew and Ricardo came back saying Sebastian we got to get back Sebastian shook his head and said ladies I must leave Mya I will see you later pulling my chin in he, kisses my lips then my forehead he shook Gisele hand and said nice to meet you. I waved bye to my baby then looked at my watch we need to get back also Gisele said so you told him about me? I was thinking should I tell her about the dream my conscious was like sure give her more ideas. I looked at her and said yes, I did why she asked because he is my boyfriend Gisele and I don't hold anything back from him I just told him I think you had a crush on me I did not mention this morning kiss. So? Did you enjoy the kiss Gisele asked I looked at the time and said we must go standing up and walking towards the exit Gisele said so you did enjoy it is that why you are not answering the question?

Exasperated I said yes I did but it won't happen again I am not going to jeopardize my relationship Sebastian and I have come a long way! In the back of my mind I was like who in the fuck am I fooling I want her to make love to me but at what cost. Damn, damn, damn my blasted ass hormones are seriously out of fucking whack I need to make a doctor's appointment a.s.a.p. We get into the elevator after a long silence between us and she does it again stopped the elevator! I said fuck Gisele I have enough of this for one day she said I am not going to touch you I just want to know if you can make a little time for me I don't need much just to see you sometimes.

Blinded by her natural beauty and sexy lips I agreed she said thank you she started the elevator and got off at my floor with me I said you coming to work with me today laughing she said no I want to see where your office is. I said hold on Gisele that's more like stalker type shit she laugh no not at all I walked into the office and Mr. Jordan still was not back I walk into my office and Gisele walked in behind me and locked the door looking at her I picked up my phone and checked my messages Mr. Jordan said he won't be back in until Monday and Sebastian called to say he enjoyed lunch I hang up the phone.

As Gisele approached me leaning on my desk she said since we can only be friends I want to kiss your lips one more time I said no but as she got closer my lips parted her tongue slipped in my mouth and we kissed this time I put my hands around her pulling her into me. I ran my hands through her hair she moaned kissing me deeper I realized I wanted her just as much as she wanted me she started kissing my neck going down kissing my nipples through my shirt moving down she got on her knees lifting my skirt I was too far in to stay stop and I parted my legs as she pull my panties to the side her tongue softly caress my clit I leaned back.

On the desk my hands in her hair I'm pulling her in my heart is racing my sex is on fire I was going to cum hard I looked at her and she is looking at me I whisper make me cum sexy she is licking me and my body started to shake I pull her head in grinding my clit on her tongue I open my legs wider so she can get all of me she slipped two fingers in me and came she sucked me till I was dry I wanted more but I knew we had to stop she kept licking I tried to push her off but she kept going getting me going again I just give in and let her make me cum again.

Gisele stood up and kissed me again and said thank you for letting me taste you I licked her lips and smiled. She said I must go I'm late walking away I said this cannot happen again Gisele and we must never be mentioned to anyone, but of course Mya you have my word so, see you sexy! right back at yah Gisele I said. As she left the office a fear ran through my bone oh fuck Sebastian this cannot get out I better not have any more dreams shit I am officially out of fucking control I let this happen in the office any one could have come in on the door was locked ok but shit she just pulled an old one, two, three on my ass she got what she wanted without a fight I could not be that damn easy am I? Shut up Conscious oh but I cannot resist yes, your ass is easy and you've been punked! 've got to keep it together I have to go to the bathroom and clean up I head to the bathroom tided up I brushed my teeth washed my face I have to get home early I need to bathe and scrub any scent of her off me then it hit me I am scared to go home I can't look Sebastian in his eyes when I got back to my desk I called Mr. Jordan on his cell what is it Mya he asked I said sir I am going to head home I feel a little nauseated!

Ok Mya forward all calls to the voicemail service and lock up I will see you on Monday. Thank you, Sir, hanging up the phone I transferred the calls and rushed out called a cab went home and hit the showers trying my best not to think about today's event I roll my eyes shit I got to go to Chuck E Cheese tomorrow washing my hair and scrubbing my skin I felt better I did not want her scent to be on me I threw the clothes in a bag to be sent off to the cleaners. My phone rings its Sebastian baby I am going to have some drinks with the fellas I will see you later. I replied have a good time honey see you when you get home that give me a little more time to myself I decided to call my best friend Tamia.Filling her in on my recent events she lives in Atlanta. Tamia answers on the second ring hey girl she said I said how are you doing I miss you I've got so much to tell you. Well Then, I am fine but enough about me give me the details of what's been going on I told her about Gisele and what happened Gasping Tamia said now I knew your ass was a freak but you done took this shit to a new level, you know you jeopardize your job and most importantly your relationship with Sebastian what if she got mad at you and decide to tell him you know females are crazy right? I said yes, I know I fucked up Tamia damn Mya she says you got to cut this shit out before it gets worse. I know I feel so confused and scared I probably need to find a new job I don't want to flinch every time I go into the building I can't believe I've went this far she seduced me and I let her.

You better tell Sebastian before her ass use the revenge tool on you and tell him she knew she could have you from the first kiss now she got something on you and she will use it to get her way if you tell Sebastian at least he knows what's up. OH, Tamia I feel like shit right now bird shit damn if I did not have you to talk to I would be going fucking crazy right now I should find the right time to tell Sebastian I don't want him to flip out and cut me and her ass beyond recognition. So anyway, how are the kids doing? Growing up fast she says, Tyler will be in high school next year. Wow time flies by so fast and that new man in your life Reggie?

We are still taking it easy Mya sometimes his ass pisses me off to the extreme but he can lay pipe oh yes lord that boy can lay some pipe so I keep him around for my enjoyment, laughing together I said see that's is why I don't talk to your ass on a regular basis her phone beeps an she says okay Mya I will call and check on you later that's Reggie on the other line. Saying our goodbyes, I hung up the phone. I wished I could talk to her some more I really needed to figure out what to do I laid on the couch flipping through channels its nine and Sebastian is not home yet about nine thirty I called baby are you ok I asked he said yeah, I am on the way I will be home in about five minutes. I got up to fix something to eat I realized since I got home I have not eaten.

Sebastian stubble through the door smelling like beers he puts his hands around my waist and gave me a kiss I smiled so we are drunk huh her mumbles out something I chuckled ok handsome I will run your bath water he said no I just want to shower I said ok sit I took his shoes off and then his clothes I got in the shower with him and washed him up as we got out I dried him up and he laid on the bed I do you want anything to eat I asked Sebastian mumbled no I cover him up and he fell asleep going back into the kitchen I made a sandwich and let the television watch me because I sure was not watching it I laid back on the couch and fell asleep a loud thump scared the life out of me and I woke up running Sebastian? I screamed are you ok?

Where were you he said angrily I said I fell asleep on the couch watching a movie I'm sorry I did not come to bed. Breathing a sigh of relief he said I reached for you and you were not there when I rolled over I almost hit the ground I rushed to his side oh baby I did not mean to scare you I did not realize I feel asleep. Well go cut the TV off and come to bed he whispered I quickly ran into the living room and came to bed he held me close and we both drift off to sleep. I got up and made breakfast because I knew Sebastian would have a hangover I did pancakes eggs bacon and sausage, brewing a fresh batch of coffee my baby strolls into the kitchen good morning honey.

I said holding his head he said I have a headache babe I had two Tylenols already on the counter with a glass of water here take these I said and sit so you can eat I poured some coffee, I want it black he says. Softly I remind him I should go to my niece party today at Chuck E Cheese the way you look right now I am sure you would want to have a quiet day, right? Speaking slowly Sebastian asked what time will it be I said at two, but I won't get there till about three thirty I just want to give my niece her gifts and come home it's been a long week. So where did you go last night baby? Eating his breakfast, he said oh we went to Maria's the Mexican bar right across the street from the Barbados Restaurant! OH, yeah right there off Pine I said, shaking his head he said yeah babe we got twisted I am feeling the pains now but there is one thing I've been thinking of doing to you all night.

And what might that be I said to Sebastian, well come close let me whisper it to you so I stand between his legs with my hand around his neck realizing how much I love him and I don't want to lose this relationship not even for a beautiful chic, nuzzling his nose I whisper whatever you want baby I will do it for you just say the word. So, he says baby I really need to hit that ass right now my dick has been hard for so go get the lube. I looked at him and said ok so I go get the lube while thinking to myself you got to get me hot for all that we did it before and after you pass the painful entry it get real good, I am not sure that I am up for this but after the Gisele encounter in my office I've got some serious making up to do, shit my ass already hurt thinking about this but I have to give my man what he wants or else he will go elsewhere to get it. breathing out a sigh, I head back to the kitchen and there he stood naked with his dick in his hand just like I like it. I said baby what exactly did you have to drink last night he some drink I can't remember all I know it was mixed with 151.

Oh, fuck I fear you now Sebastian I said come over here baby Sebastian motions to me I said you got to get me wet for the shit because I am nervous. Don't worry about all that I got you baby now take your clothes off and let me see that pussy says Sebastian I strip instantly coming closer Sebastian moves his dick up and down my clit kissing me as if he missed me so much but in a way to say I would fuck you up if you decide to fuck up but was it my imagination. Sebastian then says give me all you Mya he pulls me to the lounge chair he sits back I straddle him as I begin to sit down grabbing my ass he pulls me into him planting soft kisses around my freshly shaved sex I looked down and his eyes meet mines he's making love to my pussy nice and slow his tongue slides around sides and inside I am about to fucking bust as I look back his one hand is stroking his dick the scene was so sexy.

He lets go of his rock hard dick grabbing both of my ass checks he finger fucked hard while licking my clit I came trembling holding his head and screaming out his name Sebastian oh daddy what you do to me I want to suck you off baby let me taste you I am hungry feed me , baby I cried. Sebastian said no that's not what I want, he pulls me down on him and reaches behind me to out the television on presses play and a porn came on, I giggled oh we have not done it like this in a while, licking my neck he said we are past due baby I want to fuck you hard. Squeezing my Nipples, I teased him come on with it baby he also turns on the stereo loud to stifle noise Usher Lemme see is bumping in the background I said hold up I need a drink laughing he said go get a shot and hurry up and bring your ass back here quick.

Hoping off I said keep that dick hard till I get here! Sebastian slaps me on my ass hmm there is nothing like some morning sex he said you may not be able to make it to the party when I get done you ain't, gonna be able to walk you might need a band aid for that ass. Laughing. I said you better not I took a shot of Patron Silver it slid down my throat like hmm shit I poured some in a regular glass I might need some more of this depending on how deep you get looking at Sebastian out the corner of eyes. He said underlay Mame hurrying back over with my glass in my hand before I place it on the end table I take a swig reaching Sebastian he is watching the porn its two women eating each other as the man kneels on the bed sticking his dick into one off the women the one he is not fucking has balls on in her face as he slams the other hard that seem to turn Sebastian on?

Oh shit I am getting mixed signals here is he trying to fuck with my head I looked at Sebastian and he is really into it I said baby you like that? He said its sexy come here he says I want that tight ass of yours groaning he stands up and says kneel on the chair ass up in the air come here he says to the side, so we can see the TV. Pulling me in I can feel it as he spits and the saliva slides down my ass it's hot and wet it feels good Sebastian runs in finger around the rim where is the lube he says, picking it up from the floor I hand it to him. Baby can you give me my drink before you start I need another drink he give me the glass and this time I chuck it down making the ahhhh sound the tequila goes down and my ass goes up I'm ready baby I said.

He said now that's what the fuck I am talking about gimme that ass Mya I want it watch the TV baby he says look at the way she is eating her pussy that's what you want right I feel a finger go in Sebastian finger is playing with my clit so even though I feel a little pressure his massaging my clit with his finger is making me lose control I feel the lube and he puts some on him also. I turned my head he said no watch the movie baby I watch as one woman sucks the man off and the other is licking his ass and his balls oh yeah Sebastian says I am ready relax he says let me get this dick in. I relax as he ease the tip in his fingers are assaulting my clit which has me in distracted and feeling pressure he grinds in slowly I bend down low my tits on the chair with my ass arched I will take this punishment for all my wrong doing with Gisele I let Sebastian get all the way in and the truth is I really want to pass the fuck out pulling me in slowly he says yes baby surrender that ass to me I moaned loud panting but enjoying it then I hear a buzz it my toy to relief my pain.

Sebastian places it by clit now I am starting to move Sebastian growls yes that's want I want you to give it to me I grab my nipples pulling them and massaging my tits I scream out baby Sebastian pumps harder and harder watch the TV baby look at the way he is fucking her in her ass while the other chic is eating her pussy is that what you want tell me? I can't believe what I am hearing so I said huh! He said you heard me is that what you want me fucking you while Gisele is eating you as you fondle her tits. Sebastian slams in hard I scream out loud he slaps my ass tell me now you have been dreaming about her so somewhere in your subconscious you are thinking about having her licking your pussy so answer me now!

I said baby I don't know he says yes you know tell me now he started to fucked me hard in my ass now my pussy is soaking wet my nipples are ripe I am about to cum every which way Sebastian leans in my ear tell me now I want to fucking here you say I might give you what you want Mya I don't want to lose you tell now baby as he pants I am going crazy then he says do you want to cum I will stop now if you don't tell me Sebastian says in a deep growl I said yes I want to cum baby don't do this to me. Then fucking tell me Mya I feel my legs shake as an orgasm is about to rock the core of my body I scream yes, maybe baby I don't know.

In a deep voice Sebastian said you said yes I whisper maybe I don't know, now standing up and pulling me in hard Sebastian growls this is my ass and fucking harder and faster I cum screaming as I wet his dick he comes banging hard I can feel his sweat falling on my back pulling me in and releasing all of him he slump on the chair with me in his arms I could not move not to mention I feel all fucked up right now my mind is going crazy my heart is beating I am worried about my confession although I can just blame it on the liquor.

He eases out of me I gasp even though he make me cum through penetration my clit was on fire I put my hand down there to calm the fire Sebastian reached for the toy put it on high vibrate kissing the back of my neck and my shoulders he slide the toy between my legs I put on leg over his leg to give him free access hmm we whisper you still hungry huh must be that Patron, panting I grind on his finger and the toy I turned my back as he sits up next to me I kiss him deeply feeling his tongue in my mouth I suck as he ease the fire between my legs Sebastian slips two fingers inside my stoking my clit I am kissing him hard moaning my body is out of control as he says come for me baby I am trying baby I am too fucking hot I can't come sticking the toy inside me Sebastian slides between my legs and started sucking my clit I can feel it baby I am about to fucking explode. Slipping his hand underneath, me to grab my ass he pull me into in mouth as I look down at him and he looks at me as I started to grinned hard on his tongue pulling his head into my cunt.

My inside was heated putting my feet on the chair so my knees are in the air I caught a glimpse at the porn and the woman was getting her pussy sucked by another woman I caved in and screamed Sebastian name Cumin harder than I ever came before I looked at him he kept sucking I was panting baby stop I can't go no more shit pleas Sebastian fucking stop he eases up and I folded in fetal position on the chair Sebastian slid behind me and he said thank you baby for giving me what I wanted I said you are welcome baby you know you give me what I need and that's why I love you so much. We laid there for a while I had the urge to pee I ignore it, because I was so comfortable in his arms I said baby I got to go to the bathroom and he said me too baby I have just been too damn lazy to move.

I said shit I been too damn tired and dick whipped to move

I don't know if I will make to the party babe I just want to bathe and cuddle with you all day no interruptions. Mya that sounds like a plan but how are you going to get out of the party well baby currently I feel under the weather I will make it up to my niece next week by taking her to a movie let me call now so it does not seem like last minute. I struggled to get up limping to the bathroom Sebastian is laughing at me I told your ass you would need a fucking band aid don't fuck with the Don baby I handles mine fucking business for sure! Whatever I said more like you murder yours shit I am scared to sit on the toilet thanks to you I feel like a fucking wounded dog oh has been thoroughly fucked call that a bitch if you would! Yeah but you are my bitch baby don't you have get that shit twisted with your freaky ass it don't make no fucking sense how horny your ass be.

Oh, hell no wait a minute like you dick don't be on what is it six o clock or twelve oh clock, all I got to do is breathe fuck and you come running, Sebastian jumped of the couch and take off behind me. My limp ass started running I tried to close the bathroom door on his ass, but he busted his way through laughing out loud and trying to push the damn door he manage to get in walking up to me he said you should have ate your Wheaties sexy that would have saved you from round two. What I said oh hell no I ain't going to be able to go to work for a week fucking with you and that second round I will have to pass on that shit oh hell no back the fuck up Romeo mama is straight gutted thanks to you my name is not fucking Juliet.

Tickling me I laughed, and scream stop at the same time I got out of his hold and turn the water to the showers on we both got in. I kept staring at Sebastian he said what's up Mya why you are looking like that I said because baby I really am in awe of you I really and truly love you and I want to spend the rest of my life with you, you make me so happy I held him tight and it felt like it was almost what we both needed me realizing what I have in front of me and him needing reassurance that I will always be around. Hmm Sebastian says see what a good fuck in the ass can do for you I almost think that you need pain every now and then to bring you back to your senses even though I enjoyed every finger fucking licking and dicking part of it.

We both bust out laughing I said your ass is a comedian huh! Sebastian said go on and bend over let me hit that spot again I said hell fucking no and ran out the shower. I can hear Sebastian voice saying come back here you fucking coward laughing I said I will be that coward fuck that shit I am straight you murdered the pussy, or should I say my ass I don't need no more what I need is some gauze and duct tape to keep this shit off limits. Is that right Sebastian says I got your duct tape right her however do you want it babe I'll shut that hole tight.

That is just wicked I said you fucking freak! Sebastian say hold the fuck up Mya I know you ain't calling my ass no freak miss I want a woman to lick me while getting fucked. Ok Sebastian stop playing I was under pressure and forced to respond to you so that shit don't count.

Yeah alright Sebastian says did you call Diamond to let her know your ass has been locked down and you can't get the fuck out today? Whatever Sebastian I don't see no handcuffs smirking Sebastian says Mya don't fucking tempt me. I back off and say let me call her now! In my mind, I am thinking I should go but I can't resist a day with my man plus I feel like I owe it to him maybe sometime today if the mood is right I can tell him about Gisele. Hmm no my conscious scowls at me you better keep that info for yourself before you be singing that Bobby Womack song "if you think your lonely now wait until tonight girl" I agree and decided to shut up because this could be a doubled-edged sword, a means to an end, a big mistake or more like a dumb ass move.

It would be like I am begging to lose my relationship if it ever came to light what Gisele had done to me in the office I would deny that shit big time! The phone rings three times then Diamond answer "Mya your ass was supposed to be here by now where the fuck are you" Diamond barked, my ear drums are ringing at without thinking I said what the fuck has eaten your ass alive? You did not even let me speak and I am the one that called anyway before you say another word which will make me exhale your ass tell my niece I said Happy Birthday and I have her gifts for her and love her thank you! All I heard was bitch you better be here...... shit right then and there I hung the phone up.

Now I am pissed off thinking to myself first Diamond boo boo dear I'm too fucking fly for this kinder garden shit! Not knowing that I was talking out loud Sebastian said I guess that did not go too well smirking at him I was like you think? Anyway, I am hungry let's do a delivery order what are you in the mood for Sebastian asks I said Chinese because I feel like eating liver for not attending my niece birthday party. not like my sister gave me enough notice even with the excuse I am making, I still feel bad and I need a doctor, is there anything you can prescribe for me Sebastian? He looked at me, then cleared his throat let's see hmm, one cup and sperm that is collected my maintaining a steady sucking motion on my, I'm sorry I meant your doctor's dick that should do it also add a shot of tequila then suck on an ice cube before performing this maneuver.

And please brush your teeth thoroughly because the doctor may want to be kissed! Laughing loudly, I said ok doc can we eat first cause the patient can't get down with an empty stomach. Look on the fridge and hand me the menu for Mr. Chang's Wet Rice I'll order Mya you change the channel unless you trying to get dick in your right eye, I can do a striptease for you slide my dick up and down your face all up in them eyes girl. Laughing I said smart ass please order the blasted ass food before you make me mad, Shoot I should close shop for the day! What shop Sebastian asks, I said hmm what you say, Sebastian jumps up don't play with me Mya what shop are you attempting to close? Tell me now I want to hear you say that shit, laughing I say so here it goes you ready? Teasing him I count one, two, three and screamed de pome pome shop then I took off running the neighbors started to bang on the ceiling.

Sebastian screamed its damn near two o clock in the day bang on that shit again you will see. Still trying to run he catches me and swings me around my hand around his neck he is holding me up effortlessly in the air. Looking down in his eyes laughing and thinking to myself wow he is hot and he is mine I love me some him... by Toni Braxton here we go gotta let this one play! Pulling me down I said I want to play a song for you, so I pull out Toni CD and played track 11. I turned around and Sebastian was standing behind with his hand around my waist I place my hands around his neck tilted my head went in for those sexy soft lips. Sebastian as I kiss him softly as I pull back he whispers my name Mya repeatedly as we danced I can feel his erection, fuck the food I got premium grade A beef that I am about to devour.

As I kiss his neck I whisper in his ear I love me some you sugar now let me show you getting the whip cream and strawberries I said baby go lay on the couch, I have to follow the doctors order remember so let me prepare, placing the strawberries and whip cream on the center table I then ran off to the bedroom straight to the lingerie drawer and pull my one piece with the cut out sides, the low back cut, the fuck pumps gotta to have that thanks to Carlos Santana's shoe line. Ass hanging out the one piece one pussy lip to the side I am trying to pull her ass back in, damn unruly cunt I swear.

Quickly I pulled my hair up and put on the come fuck me like a whore/ then tip me red lipstick; I put my tongue piercing on and spray a little perfume. I head back into the living room I stood and said baby his back was turned to me as he turned around he had two shots of Patron, looking stunned he said damn Mya you clean up nice as he kisses me softly he feeds me the shot from his mouth. His tongue explores my mouth feeling the tongue Sebastian moans oh baby you did that for daddy? You beautiful, sexy, hot, always tight and wet woman of mine, you make me want to surrender all! Hmm I said you are a disgruntled doctor I told you to lay on the couch so surrender your ass in position on the couch, so I can to be healed!

Sebastian threw is hands up and says yes, the doctor is guilty as charged would the patient please find it in her heart and her tongue pierced tongue to forgive me as she punishes my grade A dick. I said stop making me laugh Sebastian this is serious! Ok Mya baby come on I will behave myself for as long as I can. I looked at him out of the corner of my eyes and smiled taking the whip cream I create a heart on his chest of course like a big baby he says oh this is cold! I said don't worry baby you will be all warm soon I take one strawberry at a time and pass it on Sebastian chest where I made the heart and feed the strawberries to him while I lick his chest always keeping fresh sprayed whip cream when the strawberries were done. I focused on his hard dick.

Sexy 4

I said sit up on the couch but slide down a little getting on my knees between his legs, spraying some whip cream on his dick I placed his dick in between my tits Sebastian starts moving oh yeah baby he whispers I moved my tits up and down going down I licked the tip of his hard dick then go down , even though I damn near chocked I held it all in because that Patron coming up would not be what's up.

Holding my breasts close to his dick I let him fuck my tits not letting him cum I pull away and sprayed more whip cream I want to build him up and stop and start over again so he can produce that fucking cup of cum. Let's go Doc I said, then he replies lets fuck patient my dick is about to explode and connect with your throat. Whatever I shrugged and spayed the whip cream high on his dick and without hesitation I deep throat that dick no coming up for air, my tongue ring ball is sliding over the tip of Sebastian raised his ass off the couch.

I can pull him in as I deep throat my tongue explores the rim of his dick and the length as I come I go down again then I pull away. Now he's cussing fuck no Mya stop this shit now you fucking my shit up what the fuck is wrong with you? I said baby I know its frustration but you said one cup of cum and that is what I am looking forward to having. Mya, he screams fuck the doctor I need to bust! Hold on baby I said putting the melted ice in my mouth I start my vicious assaults this time I am going to take it up a notch with my finger vibrator I massage his balls while I devour his dick, Sebastian is pushing my head up and down as he moves in motion the vibrator is stroking right beneath his balls that line before you get to his anus, gently I move the vibrator on the line and up on and around each ball each time I get a little closer to his ass he flinches oh shit baby you about to make me bust. I increase the sucking the movement of my finger caressing and vibrating I go for gold with a swift deep throat coming up sucking up and down, Sebastian is panting and growling really- hard the rhythm has increase dramatically shouting my name out loud MYA, MYA, MYA.

My lips tightened my tongue made her rounds around the tip of his penis as I go faster up and down feeling his legs tremble I know he is about to cum hard I slip the toy right by his anus and let it vibrate while he cum I am sucking leaning close my tits are touching his balls my finger roaming I slowed down and slowly removed all assault weapons and laid back on the floor. Breathing heavily and trying to catch his breath at the same time Sebastian quietly said My Love Mya! baby you are the best I will kill for you no one else can experience what we have here. you belong to me and I belong to you as off today let's put the past behind us and move on.

I said I love you more baby yes let's start new today! But as quickly as I said that my mind went into question mode so what has his ass been doing to say going forward? But then who the fuck am I to talk not to mention I am the one talking in my sleep. Sebastian shakes me quickly I come out of the trance what were you thinking Mya. I said I can't think I am hungry and my doctor is keeping me on a starving diet shit! Sebastian said ok let me order it should be here in 15mins once you bathe everything will be here I promise. I got up to thinking oh so I suck your dick but I need to bathe here we go my mind is out of control, so I got in the shower any way just to refresh I can hear him order I washed up damn I am soaking wet between my thighs as I think about how wet I am Sebastian comes in behind me he puts his hand around my neck.

Then down to my nipples pinching each one I throw my head on his shoulders and arch my body as the water runs down on me, feeling his hands run pass my navel I anticipate the touch of his fingers in my wet clit but he turns me around as he sits on the shower bench he lifts my left leg onto the bench grabbing my ass he started to suck and lick by sticking his hard tongue in an out my sex I'm about to cum just on seeing the length of his tongue. as he moves up and down my legs started to buckle as I throw my head back I knew it won't last long because pleasing him turns me on, hearing him groan in pleasure makes me want to cum; he is sucking me, sticking his tongue inside of me I feel his fingers slip inside to replace his tongue as he ravishes my clit.

I said damn baby you need some whip cream to go with that? He says I got your whip cream talk that shit you hear me and we will see who needs what Mya. Just for teasing Sebastian gets on his knees in the shower face straight up in the pussy I opened my legs wide so he can get it good licking my clit while he is finger fucking me I am about to explode watching Sebastian on his knees I pull his head in as I grind on his tongue as the water rolls down my body on to his I start panting and moaning loud I scream

Sebastian I am about to cum; a shiver runs through my spine.

Sebastian increases the licking going faster my body gets ready to release my legs start shaking I looked down at him he looks at me and stick his tongue out so I can see him one lick two licks three my body cave in he covers my sex with his lips licking viciously I come screaming Oh baby with tears running down my eyes my legs gave way my body limp Sebastian holds me up bent over I scratch his back as he pushes me up I quiver I can't stand so I sit on the bench and let the water hit me Sebastian high fives himself I am to fucked up to say anything smart so I let him win. Sitting back, he washes himself as I try to re-group and said baby you know you make me so happy and I really love you and only you. I could not stop the tears my voice was shaky I am fighting with my mind I can hear don't you ruin this moment let it stay as sweet as it is right now! Sebastian said Mya as he bends over and lifts my chin up and giving me soft kisses on my lips he said I love you more baby with that I stood up and kissing him and feeling his heart beat I explore his mouth with my tongue saying I love you passionately kissing him my body melts in his arms.

I am so loving this moment then I hear the doorbell baby runs out the shower yelling hold on a minute he closes the bathroom door I try to get myself together by the time I made it out I laid on the bed naked. Mya are you ok? Sebastian says. I said no you wore me out can you bring me some food please I am too weak to get up I moaned. Sebastian smirks yeah, I beat and eat that pussy up! I shrug him off and motion for him to bring my plate. Damn I am twisted laying here already tipsy in the day time, but I love it we had not have one of the all-day sessions in a while I am happy and content.

I am so glad I stayed home then the door opens baby puts the food on a tray sat it on the bed and we both ate I flick the tv on a game is on, and Sebastian motioned to leave it there to tell you the truth I really don't have the strength to flip the channel so I happily put down the remote. Continuing to eat I said baby I am going to take a nap after I eat! Mya, I will be laying right down with you baby I am done he said, yep this is what you do to me woman. Laughing I said oh I think it's the other way around, I am scared to go pee right now due to a swollen, beat up and thoroughly fucked vagina thanks to your 100% Premium Grade A+ type Dick. But Mya you know I am the man shit you better ask somebody woman Sebastian says while rolling his eyes. I said see that don't make no sense right there how you acting I got up a cleared the dishes, sitting them in the sink I'm fuck it I ain't trying to wash dishes right now my ass is going to bed. By the time I made it back to the room.

Sebastian had the tv off and the covers pulled back for me to lay down I slide in the bed getting right up underneath my baby as he wraps his hands around me I slid down to put my head on his chest wrap my legs around his and my arm around him I rub his back slowly he snuggled in and we slept. Three hours later I wake up to what the fuck I opened my eyes and Sebastian was cussing at the game let me say that again this man is cursing while I am trying to sleep. I looked out the corner of my eyes at his ass like really did you just fucking wake me up over a game on tv dude say it ain't fucking so! As I was thinking it my lips were moving and it all came out in a high pitch voice. Mya calm the fuck down Sebastian says because he can see my eyes are blood shot red and like the Leo I am I about to go in for the fucking kill, somebody please fucking hold me back is all I am thinking. And there go my conscious pick you battles Mya suck this shit up bitch back the fuck down.

69

I breathe heavily and laid my head back down as soon as I did that a headache attacked my ass fuck double whammy ain't this a bitch and a half. I said can you please get me some pain pills my head hurts Sebastian reached over kiss my forehead and whisper I am sorry I waked you baby I smiled bringing me back the pain pills I licked his palm to get the pills then he placed the glass to my lips so I can drink some water. Mya are you ok he asked I said yes. I am fine I just have a slight headache baby that's all. A I drift back into, la la land after a while when I finally open my eyes it was about seven o clock at night I smelled something cooking and it was Sebastian I got up heading to the bathroom.

Sexy 5

I brushed my teeth wash my face and put a little lip gloss on. Walking into the living room I looked, and my baby is cooking so I walked up behind him biting my lips I put my arms around him. Hey sexy he, says to me I said hey daddy what you cooking? Sebastian answered I am cooking something to keep your ass in check he grins.

I answered well that's some scandalous shit right there. We both laugh I glance in the pot and its chicken and beef fajitas with some avocado rice, flour tortilla for me and corn for him it smells delicious in here I said how much longer baby I mocked him. Listen Mya it will take as long as it needs to take so shew fly don't bother me Sebastian said waving him off I started to straighten up the living room area then the phone rings it my niece Mariah saying hi Aunty Mya I said yes baby girl happy birthday! how did you spend your day? She said I had fun at Chuck E Cheese I said great, so aunty and uncle Sebastian has, your gifts for you I will see you tomorrow okay? Mariah said gifts as in more than one yeah! Thank you, tell Auntie I love her. I said I love you, pumpkin see you soon.

All I heard was bye auntie I love you! then I can hear Diamond ass talking Mya your sorry ass should have come that's just trifling wait till you have your kids I ain't coming to none of their events I said bitch shut the fuck up will all that shit I don't want to hear that, Excuse me I am where I want to be at this moment in my life I am sick of doing what every fucking body else wants me to do so back the fuck down and shut the fuck up I yelled. Sebastian turned around and said Mya calm down walking towards me I looked at him I told Diamond get off my phone I am sorry I did not show up but I will make up to Mariah now dismiss yourself shit I am fucking pist off. I threw the phone in the corner I am mad and feeling bad I did not go but I got my man here who is so important to me I don't want to have to choose between family and him I wanted to stay here and spend time with him. Speaking of kids then it dawned on me oh shit we have not been using condoms today shit I may be pregnant?

Oh shit I need a calendar my period is due in a few days so I am ovulating oh man well fuck me running I can't believe this. Damn Baby! we have not used condoms today,

Sebastian said yes and what is the problem, well I am ovulating Einstein that's the problem hope you got pampers, wipes and milk money? Mya don't worry about what I've got you and I got us I need you to spread them hips for daddy let me feel that pregnant pussy juice! Sebastian, you just nasty, I sit back and look at my man in the kitchen cooking for me I am so grateful for him even if I got pregnant tonight I won't mind it at all. but his ass is going have to pay Gucci please forget the ring I require two purses with matching wallets a pair of shades and the charm bracelet not all at one time it can be sporadic but done within the nine months. Thanks for feeding me and the little one daddy dear I said with sarcasm. Oh don't tempt me Mya cause I can go a couple more rounds to ensure a little one is present.

I laughed I got up to go get my food and was ordered to sit back down he delivers my plate we sit everything on the center table I got down on the floor with Sebastian all we are missing is a Corona baby as I got up to get them I see him motioning to get up but I beat him to the punch I put a slice of lime on his I like mines with grenadine we ate in silence that's because the food was, so damn good. Even if I said something Sebastian won't answer it seems as if he is not breathing in between bites. The night is still young I sipped on my Corona and relaxed I made my way over to Sebastian side we toast to us. There is a knock on the door so I ran inside to put some clothes on then I hear hi Mya its Josh and Lisa, I hollered out I will be right there I throw a sun dress on and head outsides it smell good in here Lisa says as I reach over to give her a hug. Sebastian said eh hmm a why did Y'all not call before coming over?

Luckily, we just finished having sex on the couch you are sitting on dear sister. Lisa said pew and jumped up of the couch we laughed. I asked Josh if he wanted a beer before he can answer Sebastian says no they gotta go if this is not an emergency you need to call me before you come here. I said shush to Sebastian I asked Lisa is everything alright she said yes, they were just in the neighborhood I they thought they would stop by to say hi. Josh said no we are heading out, I said nonsense as I scowl at Sebastian be nice. I got some beers out Josh and Sebastian started to talk about sports while Lisa and I look through a home decorations magazine. Then Lisa whispers Mya I have not been feeling like myself lately I asked what's wrong Lisa and she said I am late for my period I said girl you better put that bottle down because you may be pregnant.

I whisper let's go to the bedroom that way these two noisy men won't be straining to hear what we are saying. We grab our beers and head to room, I looked in my panties draw and pulled out a pregnancy test I always get them when they are on sale you never know when you may need one.

Lisa here go to the bathroom and see call me once you're done we sat there waiting for I don't know how long then the line started to form oh shit Mya I am pregnant I said congratulations but something was wrong so I asked Lisa what is it she said I cheated on Josh and the condom broke so I am not sure who the baby belongs to. I said what Lisa? Are you serious oh my goodness who is the guy you cheated with? That's when Lisa face turned red she said Ricardo. I said Ricardo who not Sebastian co- worker Ricardo right? She said yes, the exact same one I fell back on the bed if only Sebastian knew he would kill Ricardo I said shit I need a stiff drink this beer ain't doing shit for me.

I told her get rid of the test take it with her so she can discard it I don't want my man to find it, walking in the kitchen I fixed me an incredible hulk, Josh and Sebastian watched me as I sashay back to the room I take a sip yes Hennessy and Hypnotic yes that's what's up! Lisa had her hands covering her face I said look first things first let's get you A doctor's appointment once we figure out what how far along you are at that time we can panic if it even warrants a panic.

When did this event happen with Ricardo she said 3 weeks ago and again last night! I am so ashamed, but Ricardo makes love to me with so much passion its effn hot in the bedroom my body just melts away with him Mya! Shaking my head, I said Lisa it all new right now, tomorrow is Sunday see if any emergency clinics are open so we can go for right now play it cool with Josh until we figure this all out.

I reached over and give her a hug as Sebastian walks in he tells Lisa get your hands of my woman we laughed at his comment. Lisa and I walked back into the living room as Sebastian made it to the bathroom I took a gulp of my drink. Lisa, I asked would you all like something to eat there is more food here? Lisa says we just ate I am going to head out come on Josh she motioned Sebastian came out the back saying damn I just left for a minute and Mya you already run the company away I said ha ha you got jokes huh! Josh got up and shook my hands and Sebastian I gave

Lisa a big hug and whisper call me I will go with you she said ok. Thank you for stopping by Y'all come back now here! Lisa giggles Mya you are so funny I will call you later, I blew a kiss at her and said later sis.

Sebastian could not help but throw in his two piece, yeah and next time call please I rolled my eyes at him shaking my head I said you just can't help yourself can you. You had to say something I locked the door and sat on the couch the incredible hulk is starting to kick in I feel a little bit fucked up. Mya, you look a little drunk you better stop drinking I like pussy responsive not dead so don't your ass fall asleep on me I want to get my dick wet one more time for the night. I said baby I don't know if I can handle all of that right now this kiddy cat is in ICU right now it needs to be revived I put the drink down. It's been well over three hours Sebastian says you should have recuperated by now so stop acting so stingy and gimme some that funky stuff.

I said whatever I got up and start putting away the food and washing dishes since my baby cooked I might as well do my share while Sebastian flips through the channels, my mind runs on Lisa damn this situation is messed up if it ever got out to Sebastian I think he will go crazy on Ricardo I'm thinking to myself damn when did they get introduced and how can Ricardo pulled that off without Sebastian having a clue wow and here I thought I had problems shaking my head I sigh damn I feel so bad for her right now this thing can go either way. Isn't this the same Ricardo who was hitting on Gisele damn I can't let Lisa know that this is too much at least it's distracting me from my own mess. Just thinking about Gisele eating my pussy my clit went into over load.

I can feel the wetness damn I feel weak I leaned over the sick squeezing my legs that damn pretty ass female I wanna fuck now so I called Sebastian baby come I bend over the sink raised my dress up panty less I say I am hot baby fuck me! his dick went from relaxed to a full attention. I leaned down on the sink so he can hit from behind he said fuck you ain't give it to me like this in a while! fuck me hard I said hit the lights thee can't see through the kitchen window, forget the neighbor.

I'm going to stand here and let you put it down on me I started fucking him and it felt good Sebastian moans damn baby this pussy so good! Tightening my muscles and releasing it I backed up on his hard dick he leaned in lifting one leg and banged his dick inside of me I screamed oh baby then he did it again grabbing me by my shoulders, he pulled he jammed into me again straight daddy long strokes.

Mya, he moaned damn you so wet I am not going to last, he whispers in my ear those words went straight to my crotch and I came! Wet me down baby he moaned sliding his finger in circles around my clit come Mya give me one more wet my dick sexy and I released again to his command. I imagined Gisele beautiful soft lips eagerly licking me and I came again fuck Mya you gonna make me come in you if you keep wetting me like that. My body started to tingle all over I turned away from the sink so I can bend down and touch my toes Sebastian is now leaning on the sink I am bent down in front of him giving him all ass I am on my heels touching my toes and he bend his knees so he can feel the tightness and wetness of my juices.

Squeezing my muscle tight around his dick I can feel his wet hands slap my ass which sends a tingle through my whole body bending down lower I place my hands on the floor in front of me spreading my legs wider Sebastian scoots down a little we are both going hard back and forth I am grinding back on his hard dick I can feel his balls flapping . Wining up on his dick as he pusher, I can hear him growl damn sexy daddy is about to bust this cunt wide open. Bust it wide open daddy I said while Cumin this is yours take it all mama wants to feel you cum in me baby, calling his name out loud Sebastian fuck me hard baby take your pussy it's all yours groaning and moaning I feel his legs buckle come for me baby nobody can fuck this pussy like you Sebastian.

Mya, he screamed don't move baby let me get this I want to be so deep inside of you when I come can you feel baby he moans. Yes, I can; I replied then thinking to myself yep I can feel all the blood running into my head also. I squeeze my muscles tight as I stay still I hear him whisper oh fuck I am about to cum stay still darling let daddy control this one touching my angles I let him get it moving faster and faster my body started to tremble I can feel him building up.

I am too oh baby I screamed I am Cumin again wet me down he growls with your sexy ass Sebastian pumped two more times and exploded my body kept trembling as he released all of him inside of me. No more I whispered I just want to go to sleep we moved to the couch to lay down both of us was weak I can barely hold up and so could he I laid there wounded I said baby let's make it to the bed we take the lights off check the door to make sure it was locked then we headed to the bedroom I really want to wash up but I can barely move so I got a wash cloth and wipe down putting hot water on the cloth when Sebastian came I wiped him down also, gentle he says baby don't wake the Lion up let his ass sleep. He has done enough exploring through your jungle for one day. I said giggling I so agree honey so let me get done quickly because I am sleepy.

Its Sunday off to go see Mariah and deal with Diamond I hope this goes well I am so not in the mood to argue with chick so I will attempt to keep my cool. Sebastian is home asleep I should be to, but I am scared he will roll over inside of me and all fucked out I don't even want to see a dick right now, I called Diamond to let her know I was close to the house. She replied oh I did not think you were coming Mya so I left I decided to take Mariah to Sears to get pictures done. I wanted to curse but I figure shit I can't always give people what they want and its obvious Diamond is looking for a reaction from me. Not today bitch you can't control my moods, so I replied ok Diamond well I will drop the gifts over Mom's house you can go get it from there! I hung up before she says anything else, damn stupid ass I swear if we

81

were not blood related I would bash her head in with a damn shovel I shouted some people are so fucking stupid! Let me calm down, breathe Mya breathe before you get a damn rash!

Let me call my Mom so I dialed her number and there is an incoming call from Diamond I rejected her call, my Mom answer the phone at this point I was so upset I said MA, how are you? I am fine Mya what's up she asked I said your daughter is getting on my last nerve can I please drop Mariah gifts over to you, so she can get it? Sure, Mya just come by baby you know Diamond is still your sister, right? I said yes Ma but right now she is your daughter I ain't got no siblings right now I am an only child. Mya stop the nonsense I will see you soon my child, stop by Mc Donald's and bring me a cup of coffee make sure they add the cream in it no sugar I will put my own! I reply yes Mom I will see you in a bit. I hung up the phone and Diamond is calling again I reject her ass because I am not going to get a hernia messing with her.

I pulled up and order two coffees I need one too shit I pulled into the driveway Mom comes outside to help me, she got her coffee and one of the bags I bought the rest in the house.

We sat on the couch drinking our coffee, Ma damn near spit hers out I said Mother you said no sugar we both laugh she said shit Mya I forgot so how is Sebastian treating you baby girl? He is taking great care of me Mama I really love him I said, yep I can tell by the way you smiling well he is a good guy you all have been together what two years now when are you all going to take the next step Mya?

Mom I am happy were we are right now I don't want to mess things up plus I want it to be his decision to marry me not me pressuring him. I don't want to push him away by giving him an ultimatum or anything like that you know? Mya that is now what I am saying you can casually bring it up I mean you want to spend the rest of your life with him right I said yes Ma'am. Well then listen Mya sometimes men need a little push to get of their ass and handle up on the business he has had you for two years and if you don't say something it will be another two years, you are thinking about having kids.

Sexy 6

Someday right? I said yes Ma'am but I did not realize I was walking into a therapy session this morning Mother! Look child you don't be a smart ass and you don't need to be just shacking up with this man he needs to make an honest woman out of you. Don't you feel like you deserve more Mya you need to test the waters see where it leads you never know maybe he is not sure how you would feel if he asks you. So, come up with a way to bring up the conversation you don't want to dedicate all this time to someone then they haul off and marry somebody else. You are a beautiful young lady you just have more values if you keep giving him the milk for free what reason does he have to fully commit? Ok I am done talking I've got to go to the mall I must find something to wear tonight for bingo. I started laughing really Ma bingo are you for real who does that?

I threw up my hands I am out of here but thank you Mom I appreciate our talk I guess I never thought about things that way all this have been food for thought thank you I give her a big hug I love you mom! I love you to Mya have a safe drive back. Heading back to the car I see Diamond pulling up although I want to get in the car and drive off I see Mariah waving hi Auntie Mya, Mariah got out the car and ran into my arms hello beautiful I said auntie got your gifts inside with Grandma happy birthday my love I gave her a kiss on her cheeks a big hug then I said call me when you open them auntie must go okay. Mariah responded I love you, Auntie thank you I said you are very welcome! I got in the car as Marian walked in the house Diamond looking at me all pist off I was like shew fly don't bother me I am not going to engage in any ruckus right now with you. I started the car as she walk up I backed out the drive way and drove off sorry boo boo no entertainment here.

Driving home I the words my Mother said to me really started to bother me she was right why have not taken another step in our relationship yes, he was talking about a baby last night but the most important step he neglected to address. Not as if I even thought about bringing it up I am just as guilty as he is wow forget Gisele I have more important things to be concerned about which got me to thinking how the hell did she get me so quickly I should have been secure in my relationship with Sebastian there was no way she should have gotten close to me. oh shit I gotta call Lisa the pregnancy drama is going to get ugly Lisa answered the phone I said I am on the way to pick you up get dress.

We went to this twenty four hour urgent care and got a blood test the nurse said the results will be back in two days Lisa and I looked at each other like shit this is going to be the longest two days. I gave her a hug I said you know Lisa if you keep that wayward pussy of yours tamed you would not be in this predicament now! Shut the fuck Mya she said laughing but Ricardo got that kind of dick that make you wanna drop your drawers at the sound of his voice. Ok Lisa that is too much damn information there but so what are you going to do if it's around the time that you and Ricardo slept together? Mya, I don't know I mean I love Josh but I got the hot's bad for Ricardo and Lord knows Sebastian will cut Ricardo ass, so yep I have issues. At the end of the day Lisa it's your life did you talk to Ricardo?

Yes, he said if it is his child he would assume full responsibility he says he wants to be with me Mya and he wants me to leave Josh. Wow yep you got a lot going on well if you need to talk just call me meanwhile I am not going to say anything you have my word. Oh, Mya I was never worried about that I trust you. We pulled in front the apartment I gave her a hug and told her don't stress it will all work itself out! Driving home shaking my head, damn I have so much to think about let me call Sebastian and let him know where I am at the phone rings I hear hey sexy in a deep voice that just melt me over the phone.

I say hey lover I just left my Mom's house I am going to walk in the park for a little bit before I get home. Are you okay Mya he says, I said I am fine I just had a talk with my Mom and I need to clear my head a little, think things through. Ok where are you Mya I said I am around the corner from our house I am going to the park on Linden drive! Ok I will meet you there Sebastian says, I said its okay baby I just want to walk a little. Mya Marie Walters, I will be there I will see you in a little bit whatever you trying to work out I want to be there with you and that's because I am in love with every part of you including your kinky freakish ways.

I giggled ok Sebastian Raul Gutierrez see you soon, I pulled up there is hardly anybody in the park I sat on the bench under an oak tree. My mind runs on Lisa I sigh hmm I've got to stay focus on my own business I see Sebastian pulling up shit that was quick what the fuck he just jumped out the bed? I hope he at least brush his teeth I might want to kiss as he quickly approached I stare at this beautiful specimen I love this man. Hey baby I got up to give him a hug with his hand in the back of my head he pulls me in for a kiss nice and minty just like I like it he held my hands and we started to walk so what's on your mind Ms. Walters I said you know my Mom asked about our relationship and when we were going to take things to another level.

He said yes and? I said we were talking about a baby last night and I got to thinking after I talked to Mom that I really don't want to be your baby mama or nothing like that I want the fairytale wedding and that wow feeling when we find out that I am pregnant not the other way around you know? Sebastian stop dead in his tracks and pulled me in front of him with his hand caressing my face he says baby you are all I want and I want to marry you I just was not sure if that's what you wanted plus we get along so well I don't want to ruin everything. I said that is exactly what I told my Mom I don't want the pressures of marriage to ruin us but deep down I want to take this chance with you I cannot see myself without you in my life Sebastian my eyes started to tear him. I mean I am in love with you and I believe in us but I don't want you to feel pressured.

Mya listen with his both hands cupping my face lets have something small and simple that way we don't put too much fuss on a big wedding I am ready I can't see tomorrow without you either I guess I got to go ring shopping I smiled we walked just hugging each other well that was not so hard Sebastian says I said no it was not and thank you for coming to meet me baby. Let's go watch a movie Mya we have been in the house all weekend lets go home and head out to the mall I said ok that will work, we can grab some lunch at a restaurant.

But before we go Mya! I said yes and Sebastian got down on his knees people are passing by and my eyes open wide he said I don't have the ring yet but will you marry me? It hit me like a ton of bricks even though we just talked about I was not expecting him to get on his knees I looked deep in his eyes and said yes, I will I got down on my knees and hugged him tight you are so unpredictable and that's what I love about you! He got up and held his hand out for me to get up the tears were in full force by this time Sebastian picks me up and spins me around whispering in my ear you are my fiancé I am so happy right now.

And so, am I said let's go home baby he kissed passionately when we finally let go there was a small crowd of people cheering for us I blushed and said thank you. Walking to the cars Sebastian says well I will see you at home Mrs. Gutierrez I smiled saying yes husband I will be home. We got to the house and got dressed so we can go to the mall I got a little suspicion but I am not going to say anything Sebastian kept telling me not to take too long to get dressed so I hurried up and out on some sexy jeans with a cute shirt and my wedges spray some perfume on and we were on the way Sebastian looks as sexy as he can look right now with his Marc Jacobs shades on I placed my hand on his lap as we drive who knew after all the sexing we did last night that today would be engaged Baby Face is playing on the radio "Someone Like You" my baby starts singing I glance over lovingly at him squeezing his leg I hum to the song swaying back and forth enjoying the breeze blowing through my hair we are so much in love right now everything is like rice and gravy.

I love it he is the rice and I got his avy, I could wet him up with my biscuit. Sebastian said so Mya what cut of diamond would you like? I blushed and said I love the Princess Cut baby! The Princess Cut huh hmm well I need something

90

that's fit for a Queen so I may have to do some magic Sebastian says! I interrupted baby I will be happy with whatever you give me IF I got you as my husband nothing else even matters. Please believe that you are my dream come true Sebastian we get along well even when the little things irritate us we never go to bed angry at each other although we might be pretending sometimes that we are not mad the makeup time always seem to convince us its ok we are humans and no one or no relationship is perfect.

I know that sometimes people in the public eye describe their relationships as being great all the time the truth is that is a façade we agree to disagree and that's the way of life. At the end of the day we keep it one hundred no matter the circumstance and baby that is what I love about you, I've learned to put the toilet seat down but in the back of my mind I really want to throw some cold water on your ass so can feel how my backside feel when I sit on the cold commode but Mama told me to pick my battles but one of these days I might go left hope you still love me! Sebastian started to laugh I will keep in mind putting the toilet seat down baby because I don't want you to go left on me that means no cookie and Daddy can't live without that sexual healing and that Mya is the gospel according to the late

Marvin Gaye.

We pulled into mall and my heart starts beating fast I said so what movie are we going to see baby? He said we will see what is playing when we get there in the back of mind I am thinking I don't really want to see a movie we need to go pick our rings out. But I hold my tongue and calmly let him run the show. We started to walk towards the movies holding hands I start to relax and then Sebastian says let's make a pit stop first so I said ok you lead the way I will follow. we head into the jewelry store and my heart really started to race inside I was jumping for joy my baby never disappoints me I am glad that I kept my thoughts to myself and not ruin a good time. The store manager greets us asking how can she help us today and Sebastian says that he would like to see the Princess cut engagement rings the store manager looked at me and I smiled she said ok follow me and have a seat please. She said my name is Daniel and you are?

I am Sebastian and this is my fiancé Maya she shakes our hand and pulls out a tray of beautiful rings I am trying my best to stay in the moment but I am trying to figure out how am I going to slip away to buy some lingerie for tonight this deserves an award winning session staying focus my baby picked out some rings for me to try on the all look beautiful but this one stood out the diamonds were flawless and the ring fit perfectly I love this one I whispered. Sebastian said yes it looks beautiful on your finger the store manager said well its two carat Princess Cut Halo Diamond wow it beautiful I said so how expensive is it Sebastian said excuse me don't you have to go get those shoes you wanted? I looked at him to say no but then I remember I got to get some lingerie, so I say oh yes sure I will meet you by the movies in say thirty minutes?

The manager nods at Sebastian and he said yes thirty minutes is good I gave him a peck on the lips and left and haul ass to this exotic shop that has risqué lingerie I got to get sexy but nasty with this one I started to look around and I picked out this strappy fishnet teddy and a cut out body suit that was crotch less hmm yeah ok let's pay its been about twenty minutes and I ask the clerk where are the gather belts at she directed me I also picked up some thigh high fish nets, I might just wear those with some fuck me pumps and nothing else on the clerk rang everything up now I headed back to meet Sebastian I stuff my bag in my Gucci bag walking fast I can see him so I waved to him he has this big ass smile on his face and I am smiling too because he does not have a clue what I got in store for him I am saying literally no really I mean like fucking literally shit it's about to be on like popcorn and the freak has arisen!

I ran up as I got closer and give him a hug while trying to feel if he is aroused I get real close to him I said do you really want to watch a movie baby? While grinding on him in an inconspicuous way, he said well we been in the house all weekend and you know what happens when we are home I thought you might want to get out for a minute. I said yes sure but to be honest after the day event I really want to go home and make our own movie like right now! Is that right he said! Sebastian I said that's what's up baby so what you want to do it all up to you! Mya the choice is easy let's go I want to see how this movie comes out you might have to call in tomorrow with all that shit you talking to me right now! Laughing I said shit you might have to call in tomorrow by the time I put the smack down on your ass while you are talking all that shit Mr. Man you should know Mya is in charge you better ask somebody sexy.

Damn baby Sebastian says you like the hottest I love the

way you handle things Mya I am so serious when I say I cannot see my life without you in it not like you make it easy to let go anyway! Like who is going to suck me off like you do? I said what? shut the fuck up are you serious I am just good for head baby okay keep talking that shit oral sex is going on fucking strike! Is that right Mya I bet I can make you change your mind! I said maybe you think you can with all the smart talking! We walk to the car and I am currently thinking of a master plan what should I do when I get his ass alone should I make his ass beg for the pussy or should I suck him until he is ready to climax then pull back and walk away I am so up to no good right now because baby talking shit.

Sebastian says Mya what are you thinking about I can tell your ass is up to something whatever it is make sure you have a plan B because you know I am always ready to play! I said oh but baby I am not thinking about anything at all I just want to get home and relax but we should pick up something to eat before we get home so that we don't have to cook looking at me Sebastian says ok Mya so what do you feel like eating I said baby I don't know we can do some Mexican or Caribbean food its does not matter to me or you know what we can do the Thai restaurant close to home the one that we have been wanting to try maybe if it's not crowded we can stay and eat that will be a nice engagement dinner then later you will be my desert what do you think about that? Tempting Mya lets skip dinner Sebastian said with one raised eyebrow! I said look we gotta eat to be able to endure the race I need you to beat it up like its new pussy you getting, because while I slipped away I got this cream that makes the pussy tighter than it currently is I mean like virgin sex what you trying to do? We got to eat baby now let's go so we can hurry home I might be having a sick day tomorrow if you beat the beat up too much! Laughing Sebastian says come here sexy let's go eat you got me like a fiend let's get this shit to go I want you naked pronto Mya...hmmm. Impatient aren't we honey truly we can make it through a nice dinner I promise to be good at the table no freaky stuff. Mya you better stop fucking playing Sebastian says I know you better than you know yourself you are getting ready to do something nasty but I ain't playing with you tonight so stop it! Whatever I said we walked and the waiter asked how many I said two in the private room reservations under Mrs. Gutierrez considering Sebastian eyes I am pleading to him please don't fuss let's just enjoy this my gift to you for wanting to marry my crazy, sexy ass! I said and his expression change to warmth and shock like he did not believe that I set this up and we were together the hold time.

Sebastian pulls me in his arms and whisper Mya how did you pull this off? I thought you said you had to answer your work emails you, sexy ass liar I should just spank your ass right now! Right now, baby I whispered in a seductive voice. Sebastian pulled me a way and stared at asking Mya whatever you are up to cut it out the waiter ushered us to the small private room beautiful with fresh flowers, a gorgeous dining table laid out with food and wine dining fit for a King and a Queen. We sat down and began sampling the fruits I am thinking to myself how can I catch his ass off guard ok let me see let's-drink before I do that confirm a cab will pick us up because this champagne is going to light us up tonight shit I guess no work tomorrow! I give the address to the clerk ok so we are good to go lets party baby before I came back to the room I changed into one of the lingerie I bought I put a long sweater over me that buttons down the front, I slipped around Sebastian giving him a kiss on the cheeks before I sat down.

Licking his lips and looking me up and down Sebastian says

so I see you have changed Mya I like the sweater! I said hmm well I am sure what's under the sweater will be a sweet surprise my dear fiancé so what shall we eat as I playfully bat my eyes. There is a knock on the door upon our command they entered with our dinner, desert and a bottle of champagne I am thinking I better eat or else it might be some shit coming out my mouth tonight so I will go slow stay focus Mya he should not have to drag your drunk ass out of here it should be the other way around.

We toast and I sip and put my glass down Sebastian drunk his glass and was pouring more I said wow baby let's eat first I don't want no limp meat tonight I need that frozen firm so stop drinking until we have eaten. Mya, I am fine he says just relax and enjoy this moment with no reservations we may not be going to work tomorrow due to that stomach flu that you passed on to me IF we can get home we good! I said I took care of that the cab will take us home, anyway can you please do me a favor and hit the do not disturb switch by you and the one that says lock doors.

Let's eat! Hmm what do they have Mya it all looks delicious Sebastian says a variety I said let's try small portions of everything. The food was excellent we ate our bellies full sitting back trying to digest our food we lift our champagne glass and toast to a beautiful day and new beginnings we kissed softly and passionately that the fire started to burn, my plan is about to be put into motion. So, I take a swig.

Sexy 7

Of my drink and walked behind Sebastian chair I refill his glass and mines because I will need it. I placed my hands on his chest while I kiss his neck he rests his head on my shoulder as I kiss him softly on his lips sliding my tongue in and out as I rub his chest with my hands I move my hands down to feel his Rock-Hard dick hmm I said that is what I want to eat right here and I grabbed a hold firm but gently. Taking another drink, I slide under the table Sebastian says no Mya they can come in and what about cameras?

By the time he finished his award winning speech. I had already have him in my mouth I pulled the table cloth over my head I made him scoot up the chair I go on good then the door rings I said answer tell them I am in the bathroom get another bottle of champagne! no more drinks Mya we have a half a bottle left I said ok you will regret that then tell them to take the dirty dishes and leave us alone the way the table was Sebastian back was up on the wall and he is facing the door so he can see who comes in and out but right now since I am on my knees licking his balls my ass is towards the door if a strong breeze blow the waiters might be try to attack my goodies I am all wide open and so is my man, his legs all shaking I know he wants me to stop but this is called torture and pleasure right now Sebastian is hoping the waiters would hurry up and leave he starting to tell them you know what leave those and those glasses we are still using those just leave thank you and close the door.

With that I increased my torture it's all deep throat from this way onwards I started moaning when I heard the door shut Sebastian move the table cloth so he can see my face I stared hungrily in his eyes I motion for a shot he quickly gave it to me I stop sucking took the shot but instead of swallowing I started to suck Sebastian off with the liquor in my mouth the noises he started to make were so loud an sexy deep groans. He started to move up and down with his hands gripping firm to the table I devoured his groin searching for the missing gold I sucked with no mercy looking at him every now and then to see he is always looking at me when I look at him it intensifies the feeling.

I am about to explode I am not being touched. I whisper cum for my baby as I took all of him in my mouth he puts his hand on my head pushing me up and down as he grinds his dick in my mouth, I lick the rim of his dick when he pulls me up on him I can feel his legs tremble as the motion increase faster and harder he grind I feel his knees weakened and I can hear it in his voice he is about to climax he rocks back in the chair and started to repeat my name. OH, yes with a smile on my face I am really getting it now I feel a gush in the back and my throat!

And no matter how much women they love that feeling they ass is lying to taste and feel it hit the back of my throat you must know I love your ass boo boo so release all that for me I am going to try not to throw the fuck up I said to myself. Yep a bitch got issues my conscious reminds me real live issues I responded to my thoughts. Now that my taste test has been completed I take another shot and sit back in the chair.

I really want to smoke a cigar or something but I can't we got to make it out of here so I get myself together and say are you ready for me to call the cab so that we can go home and pick up where we left off? Mya yes let's go home I am already starting to feel tipsy he says while swaying a little too much to the left. Sebastian, I cannot carry you up the stairs so please try to stay awake until we get home its only two blocks away and the cab is outside so hang in there with me a little longer ok they packed us bags to go including the a complimentary bottle of champagne it's in the cab already so let's go.

I settled the tab ahead of time. We got into the cab and the driver was playing up tempo music and Sebastian was singing along before you knew it we were home I took the bags up settle the cab and ran upstairs Sebastian was waiting by the door looking all angry I quickly defuse that.

Excuse me Mr. Sebastian is there a problem you want to discuss with me I can see that something is on your mind please don't let anything ruin our night tonight please it is important to me that we enjoy tonight to the fullest these are our memories at stake here baby A smile soften on his face I said okay now let's take a shower together and go to bed unless you want me to fix you something to eat so can sober up a little?

No Mya lets go to bathe and go to bed we lock the house up and head to the room I am thinking I hope you know my ass is on fire but I am afraid he is going to fall asleep on me we jump in the shower and began to soap each other up washing each other Sebastian says open your legs me let me wash you up I giggle and let him he washes me front to back.

While he is doing that I am holding his semi hard dick in my hand massaging it with my soapy hands, I can feel it getting harder so I leaned in to kiss him as he washes between my legs the water feels so good falling on us we rinse up and head to bed still wet se slid under the covers.

I slide on top of Sebastian I whisper in his ear don't fall asleep baby my pussy is on fire and I need you to get me off! Mya come sit on my face and me dry that wet cunt Sebastian says I felt a jolt go through my body I can feel his hands pulling my body up I sit up and moved to were his lips are straddling over him my hands are on the head board I can feel Sebastian hands on my ass pulling me in position; the anticipation of his tongue in my clit started to heat up the first lick I look up to the ceiling I know I am not going to last but I am going to try.

OH, baby I groaned I looked down at him as he sucks the lining Oh fuck I whisper he looks up and me, I started to pull on my nipples now I am moving my pussy up and down his lips oh damn baby this feels so fucking good I screamed Sebastian lifts me up so as he stick his stiff tongue inside of me fucking me with his tongue I squeezed my nipples harder I am so hot baby I feel like my body is on fire I said.

Sebastian says you taste fucking delicious Mya should I make you cum now? I begged please daddy make me cum I can't take it! Hmm Mya I think I can make you wait get on your knees facing my feet. Baby no please I want it like this Sebastian please. Mya, I am the one doing the licking so you don't have a say now I want to lick your ass and finger fuck you before I make that clit climax so move your ass in position. I pout and do as I am told quickly I can feel Sebastian move on the bed he slaps my ass I jumped because I was not expecting it. Put that ass in the air just like that baby arch your back for daddy yep just like that Mame let me see everything I feel his finger slide from my wet sex to my ass my knees went week. OH, baby I whisper? Yes, Sebastian replied.

I said I love the way you make me feel! Oh, Yeah, he responds, I said fuck yeah! Tell me that again I want to hear it! Sebastian, I love the way you make me feel you know ah oh yeah baby when oh when ah aw, ah, ah when you are fucking me, and tasting me it make me want to oh damn baby you, wrong for this shit stop teasing me make cream for you baby! Sebastian say yeah keep talking slide your ass up a little bit and talk to that hard dick with Sebastian under me I slide up a little taking him in my mouth with no hands I began my payback hmm one of my biggest asset or should I say my assault weapon emphasis on ass-au-bae. My head is between his legs, his head is in between my thighs as he licks from my sex to my ass and back again I am panting and sucking I feel like I am about to combust I started moving then he flipped me over, now I am on the bottom he is on the top he pushes his dick in an out of my mouth as he buries his head in my sex.

Sticking his tongue in an out I started getting really wet hmm baby Sebastian says wet me down he licks up to my clit and I know I am about to fucking explode I am grinding my pussy all up in his mouth stay right there baby I said as I sucked his dick my hands are on his ass pulling his dick in I feel I am about to cum; I look up taking his dick out of my mouth with my hands I kept stoking it up and down never letting go I am trying to concentrate because I am about to cum I can feel it I screamed please baby stay right there don't move oh yes baby! Starting to lick his balls while moving my hand up and down his shaft I move up to lick his ass he started to grind on my tongue while taking all of me in his mouth his stuck in tongue inside of me again I moaned loudly baby stop playing I am licking and sucking his balls gently I can hear him moan in ecstasy I open my legs wide, putting them up in the air.

Mya he whispers as I keep sucking him off he gets deeper in me as I grind hard on his lips my pussy is too fucking hot baby I can't cum fuck! But Sebastian kept going he started to finger fuck me as he licked my clit moving his fingers from inside of me he slid them in my ass and I came screaming, panting loud, my legs were shaking out of control oh baby I screamed Sebastian kept sucking Please stop baby I begged my legs are out of control now I can't take his licking I had an orgasm I manage to wriggle my way out because he had me pinned down I immediately got on my knees on the ground and started sucking Sebastian off and I can do that without any wondering hands I am done I don't want to be touched the pussy has vacated the building!

OH, no I am not done with you yet Mya come here I want to feel your wetness on my dick he pulls me up on him come on baby you know what I need Sebastian said. Now go get that tightening cream you were talking about let me see how that works Mya! I said ok your wish is my command Sebastian I whispered even though I want to roll over and go to sleep. I know if I don't handle my man, someone else will so I muster up the strength to handle the business. I got up and got the cream Sebastian sat at the edge of the bed and told me to lay down he took the cream read the instructions and applied the cream in me I open my legs and watch him smiling I said so is there a waiting period he read the tube again it says wait few minutes Sebastian says. Sitting on the bed with his feet on the ground I stood up and straddle him, taking all of him inside of me I sit all the way down on his Rock-Hard penis I place my hands around Sebastian neck he moans cupping my ass with his hands he began to pull down gently, on his bent tip dick. Damn Mya its tight I can feel it! Yes, baby I said ,and it feels so good I am riding slowly tightening up my muscles as I go down.

Damn Mya you are soaking wet and I fit tight like a glove inside of you right now and I love it baby I love you give it to me baby, cum on my dick for me I want to feel the warmth, wet me down sexy Sebastian says, my panting got louder hearing his voice my legs started to tremble. Cum for me Mya he demanded, and my legs gave way Sebastian squeeze my ass tighter pulling me down harder on him as I came I screamed out Sebastian, I pushed him back on the bed with hands on his chest I push back Sebastian has his hands on my hips pushing me back and forth this feeling is insane Mya we always have the best sex damn baby I am about to cum in your pussy don't move let me get it from here. I said ok baby I will stay still it's your pussy baby take all of hit. Sebastian screams out Mya as he pushes me harder.

Take your pussy daddy it's all yours I whisper fuck it like you want to baby gimme ALL your dick I groaned Sebastian is going crazy growling loudly stay still for me sexy he says let me get this pussy like I want it Mya. He slaps my ass hard again and again pushing me down on him as he grinds up in me the intense heat started to rise and I came again I screamed oh baby I'm Cumin Sebastian flips me over his hands gripping the bed he pushes up inside of me hard and fast I open my legs wide to give him all access as he slams into me I push down I can feel the sweat of his face on me I look up and his eyes are closed licking his lips he says you ready for this baby I say yes he said well open your mouth, I want you to suck my dick as it cums, open your mouth Mya let me see your tongue, stick it out for me yeah just like that, lift your head sexy here it come Sebastian pulls his dick out of my sex and pulling my head up he sticks his dick inside of my mouth I started to suck pulling him Sebastian pushes in and out pulling my head in with every motion.

I feel him tense out as he releases and cums, in my mouth chanting my name over and over again. I kept sucking until I felt him go limp we both laid on the bed I can't move so I pull the cover over us and went to sleep the alarm goes off damn it feel like I just closed my eyes two hours ago I am so exhausted. Mya are you up? Sebastian says I said yes baby but I don't know if I can make it in today I feel so tired! What about you honey how are you feeling? I feel like shit right now Mya; my head is banging from the damn champagne I am not going into today I will just use my sick time give me the phone Mya let me leave a message. Reaching over for the phone I said I have sick time also but I am scared if both of us stay home neither of us would get any rest, you know you and your trigger happy dick always trying to bust in something! Laughing Sebastian says Mya your ass is crazy funny that's why I love you like who the fuck says those things you do? You should be writing A play or something you got a natural talent. Ha Ha Sebastian you got jokes huh!

No Mya I am so serious go-ahead girl go make daddy some money! Here is the phone make your call, so I can make mines! What Mya you are a brave girl you are calling in sick with me well that's a first I almost feel sorry for you, but I will let you learn from your own mistakes. Sebastian what the hell are you talking about I said what mistake? Mya, you think I ain't gonna try to fuck if you stay home with me I hope you can hang! Is that a threat Mr. Gutierrez because I don't take treats lightly just in case you did not know? Let me make my call Mya I got something for that ass today you might want to do the right thing and go to work. I let him make his call and I am trying to figure out if he really wants me to go or if this is a challenge because I am always up for a challenge he better as some body. I made my call sounding pitiful as fuck I am sure Mr. Jordan is worried about me.

I was trying to get out the bed when Sebastian pull me back down I said stop baby I gotta go pee he said oh is that right well let's see how good you can hold your bladder I said Sebastian don't you play with me I will pee on your ass I am so serious with that I felt a push and he was inside of me my eyes opened wide, my mouth was open I was in shock! Mya, you are catching flies or what close your mouth and oh yeah hold that pee I don't want a prissy dick today! I said fuck you Sebastian get off I manage to pull and away I took off running to the bathroom and locked the door and I could barely make it to the damn toilet as soon as I sat down it came down I sat there for a minute just trying to catch my breath and come with a plan to attack if needed I decided to take a shower since last night we fell asleep after sex I was too exhausted to get up which reminds me I need to change sheets also today it's been a lot of sexing going on maybe I will get some cleaning done as well freshen up the house.

I did all my shaving when I was in the shower and now off to make so breakfast for my hubby by the time I got out the shower Sebastian had fell back to sleep I slipped into some boy shorts and a short t- shirt no bra I slipped my house shoes on and head to the kitchen started on the bacon and links I cut up the peppers, onions and tomatoes for the omelets. Getting the pancake mix I whip up some batter while humming in the kitchen I feel soft hands reached around my waste I look around my man is behind me whispering you not going to leave me hanging are you baby I smiled and said I got you baby but let me feed you first I softly bite the bottom of his lip so do you want orange juice or coffee? I will take some coffee baby let me help you I will get the coffee started Sebastian said I rolled my eyes hmm everything has a price I said so you are helping me what is the catch? Because judging from the comment you made in bed about you got something for my ass I am interested in knowing what your motive are?

Well Mya you worried about the wrong things Sebastian says stop worrying about my motives and what I am up too! You just need to know that I always got you covered sexy! Yeah um hmm ok! Sniffling I said I smell game but I am ready so if you want to play we can play but let me finish cooking breakfast. Can you set the table please babe I said to Sebastian! Certainly, he replied as he winks his eyes, I said don't you even try it, shaking my head I finish the eggs and started on pancakes everything is almost done I fixed the plates sitting them on the table I place the pancakes in the middle of the table we sat down blessed the food and ate I catch myself staring at him and smiling he tilts his head to the side and said what are you thinking in that pretty little head of yours Mya?

Blushing I said oh nothing at all I am just enjoying my view if you don't mind? Sebastian smiled yes, I know I am a sight for sore eyes! You are so conceited I said it's just ridiculous, but I love every little bit of it, you know like I really love you! And I love you my Queen you are my everything so hurry- up and eat and you will be rewarded properly! I laughed whatever, rewarded properly who says that? But on a serious note baby I really want to do some cleaning up and rest today I need to change the sheets on the bed and stuff so the sooner we can get the things accomplished is the sooner we can get our groove on so don't even! Don't even what Mya?

I said Sebastian don't even try thing let's take care of home then we can chill and watch porn for the rest of the day for all I care! Look Mya all I ask is that you put some of that tightening cream on and position your ass on this dick and we can go from there! I said no I will put my clothes on to go to work right now Sebastian and I am not playing. Calm down Mya eat your breakfast baby you going to need your strength and you already called into Jordan, so I know you don't want to go in unless you trying to see your lesbian lover what's her name again jezebel or Gisele. I was like what my lesbian lover wow baby I think you have gone too far with that one! Did I go too far Mya? Tell me because I want to know do I worry about you sneaking off to get licked by a bitch? Okay Sebastian wait a minute where are we going and why are we having this conversation we just got engaged yesterday never mind I don't have a ring on my finger right now, but we are moving forward so let's get everything out in the open before we move forward apparently you have concerns so let's talk about it.

You want to know if I would run off with Gisele the answer is NO so you don't have to worry about her. Mya did you ever have sexual relations with that woman? Are you, serious right now Sebastian? Yes, I am so answer the fucking question and don't lie because I already know the answer! Well since you already know the answer why are you asking you want confirmation I will give it to you so whatever your answer is in your head you are correct! Now what you got to say about that? And OH, remember we are starting new forget the past now that you got me on blast tell me what are you hiding? Oh, no sexy stop the fucking presses! Before you move on to me, tell me when this thing happened with you and Gisele? I never said anything happen Sebastian I said whatever you think! Mya try not to get your ass fucked up today there are no neighbors home everyone is at work except nosey Rosy.

On the first floor so fuck all this cleaning you trying to do we need to have a discussion because your ass talks in your sleep so will let me know what the fuck is going on now. My heart hit the floor I am trying to keep a straight face but now I am scared but I am not giving away shit I am going to fight this tooth and nail. I got up and got the dishes I walked to the kitchen and when I turned around Sebastian was on my heel. I place the dishes in the sink he reaches over me and put his dishes down I am facing the sink and he is behind me his hands on my shoulders answer Mya! I said let's sit down please?

He lets go off me walking to the couch I am coaching myself in my mind not to say anything turn it around on his ass. Before I can even lie he says ok it's in the past but if we are going into marriage we need to be honest with each other and I will be honest to anything you want to know I will answer. I thought about what he said and at this point there is no use in keeping a secret. I said after we all went to lunch Gisele followed me to my office when we got off the elevator she said she can see how in love we were and that she does not want to come between us and that she just wanted to kiss me and before I can say no her lips were on mine she began to kiss my neck before I know it she was on her knees and tasting me I could not stop her at that point and that's the only time that happened it will never happened again I have regretted it since and that's the whole truth baby I did not know how to tell you.

Sebastian screamed I knew it you kept mumbling in your sleep and could make out her name. Immediately tears started to run down my eyes I kept saying I am sorry! Mya, I knew that there was some attraction there, but I did not think you would let it go this far and in your office if you had gotten caught you would be fired. I know I said I was not thinking at all I should have known better I am thinking of looking for another job I don't want this to come between us I made a bad decision. Yes, you did Mya but somehow, I am happy it was with a woman and not a man, speaking of men has you slept with any other man while we were together?

Sexy 8

I said Hell No! it's been two years and Gisele is my only fuck up and not like you give me a chance to have sex with any other man anyways not the way you keep me dick down. Tears still rolling down my eyes because at this point I don't know if I was tricked into telling him what happened or was I really talking in my sleep either way it's out in the open now and I don't have to carry this burden to my wedding ceremony.

So, I said ok I was honest is there anything you want to tell me Sebastian he said well I might as well let you know that last year when I went to spend some time with my father when he was sick my ex-girlfriend came over to see me at Dad's house, I said ok and what happened? We went out for drinks and one thing lead to another she slept over my Dad's house with me I was out of it babe! Ok so you were out of it what you can't remember what happened?

Wait a minute is that the same night you said you was over you cousins and your battery for your phone died all that time you were fucking? Well we were both naked when I woke up, so I am sure the unthinkable happened Mya! Wow I said damn ok, so this is all in the past is there anything else Mister? Well Mya I got this chic at work flirting with me, but I don't want her. I said I will kick her ass who is it?

What's her name? Sebastian starts laughing maybe we should hook her and Gisele up since they trying to break up a happy home. Laughing I said hey that's a good idea because this weekend put everything in perspective for me baby and no matter of our short comings and lack of better judgment I don't want to be without you I see you in my life for always let's promise to work through the bullshit and be real with each other going forward I don't want to dwell on what happened when you were away at your Dads even though now any time you go home I will be accompanying you. And you don't have to worry about Gisele I give you my word if it gets crazy I will find a new job or let you talk to her since she might think that she has that incident over my head.

She does not have a clue that you know I am not proud of that at all but I am not going to beat myself up over it I just want to keep growing with you and I am so happy we can talk like this. Thanks for not choking me to death baby! Oh!

119

Mya, I have another way to punish your ass and I don't want to hear no complaints at all!

I will take any punishment you give me baby and while you at it don't forget I should punish you as well only you may not be so happy about my punishment, the say absence make the heart grow fonder we will find out if that is a true statement Sebastian. Don't fuck with me Mya because I am going to always win this game I am a man and you are my woman slash fiancé and soon to be wife you better read that submit part over and over again, until you get it! Submit????? Is that what you just said Sebastian?

That's right wife submit to your Husband I know you heard that before Mya come on now stop acting like you brand new and shit recognize the cliché if you will! Recognize the pussy will be on strike while you are waiting on me to submit if you will! Keep talking that shit Mya don't forget Papi got the put your ass to bed dick so if want to be sitting up late nights please be my guess and don't submit let me know how that shit turns out for you. Yeah ok we shall see Papi! I said. So, Mya you want to play your call I will sit here and watch this porn and jack my dick off and no matter how much you beg me I won't touch you or let you touch me.

Okay then Sebastian I will sit right here while you are jacking off and use my toy to satisfy myself I might even finger fuck myself. Mya, I will tell you what you can do all of that and I promise you at the end of it all you will submit to me so we can waste time doing this or we can get to the good part when I fuck that tight pussy with my crooked dick.

I say we got a challenge and I bet I will win not put your money where your mouth is how much cash you got right now I will match that? Sebastian says Mya, Mya I warned your ass to go to work, but you did not listen I have a hundred dollars where is yours? I said ok let me see I reach for my purse I only have forty- five dollars shit! Okay I got forty- five dollars cash and fifty-five, on my debit card. I accept it Sebastian says now let's go you want to be a bad bitch show me what you got today I told you that you should have taken your ass to work but no you want to ramp with the big boss, you going to be begging me Mya I can feel it.

You better bring your A game Sebastian with your Grade A type Beef and that is whilst you are talking mega shit! I said with a smirk. Okay so let's hit the showers together Mya, I said no is that a way to get me to start begging you nope I will pass sir! Get your ass in this shower with me now Mya! Ah NO! that is called submitting to your request which I refuse! Now on to the next one what else you got baby? I will beat your ass that is what's next Mya, I laugh ok well I already took my bath this morning when you were asleep.

I will be fingering my pussy or is it your pussy until you get out of the shower so hurry up dear! I waved him off putting in a movie this going to be fun I straighten up a little. I lit a few candles I put the surround sound on soft music playing in the background while sex movie is on I run in the bedroom and put on my gather belt with my thigh highs stockings no panties on and a bra that has the nipples out and the sexiest accessories of them all my come fuck me pumps, shit where the hell is my toy I am trying to hurry up because I hear the water turn off in the shower shit ,shit where is it I reach my hand under the pillows yes I found it, quietly I head out into the living room where it nice and sexy I got the curtains closed the candles lit and the tv going I position myself on the couch I got up and pull the coffee table so I can rest my legs on it. I hear Sebastian open the bathroom door. Glancing at the TV the woman is licking a woman sitting on the bar while a man is standing behind her with his dick in his hand slapping her ass I move my hand up and down my crotch and moaned. Mya, you could not wait for me Sebastian said. I did not answer I just kept on then I thought about it we still have champagne even though its only eight in the morning I got up and took a swig from the bottle and hurried back on the couch the door opened as soon as the man when inside the woman she is still licking the other woman Sebastian walked up to me and I kept playing with myself and moaning leaned over and whispered oh baby two can play this game tell me when you ready to stop and submit.

I rolled my eyes and him and whispered never! I will not give in let me remind you that I have all day to play baby so however do you want it we can do it. It's your call Mya don't forget that! Sebastian place a towel underneath him and sat down with his dick in his hand I am trying not to watch him because that turns me on and he knows it.

Sitting on the recliner he pushes it back and sits his feet on the foot rest I look over at him and I lick my lips sticking my finger in and out of my sex I moaned his name seductively Sebastian I repeated when he looked over at me I pulled my fingers from inside of me and put them in my mouth hmm

I groaned as I suck them then I stuck them back in I scoot down on the couch putting my feet on the coffee table my knees are in the air and I turn to where Sebastian can see what I am doing. I am working one finger inside of me and the other hand are pulling on my nipples one at a time Sebastian is watching me and I can see him at attention hmm I daddy you want my lips to come, lick the pre-cum off the tip of your dick? Fuck Mya you know I want you to, but I am good I got this dick you handle you!

Are you sure Papi you know you can stick it down my throat, so I can make it cum like you like it? I can see his hands moving faster I am getting heated myself as I look at him I start to move faster around my clit then I reach for the toy I looked at Sebastian as I turned it on I focus on the movie and the man was hitting the woman from behind she had one leg on the bar and one leg on the ground while he fucked her his hand massage her clit. You could tell that she was about to release I put my wireless headset on so I can hear the TV and so did Sebastian but what I like about these headsets is that we can hear each other talking or making any noises. I can hear her moaning in the movie I started to moan I can hear Sebastian say damn baby can I get it like that? I opened my legs wide using my toy I start grinding on it I whisper oh Papi I screamed Sebastian says yeah baby talk to me! I said I am about to cum baby come over here and taste me.

I want to Mya, but you got to tell me that you will submit. OH, but baby look at the way he's fucking her come fuck me now I want you! I said. Did you say you will submit Mya? I said no I am about to cum and I screamed in ecstasy as I came I can hear Sebastian panting in my ear oh fuck Mya oh fuck watching you cum made my dick so fucking hard come sit on it mama? I said nah your ass did not want to come taste me before I came and even if really wanted you too I won't. Come on now baby you gonna give me blue balls, I laugh blue balls really baby we fuck too regular for you to have blue balls I am not falling for that one.

Mya just feel it come on girl it won't hurt you! Ha, ha, ha you got jokes but I am not coming to feel anything so feel free to make it happen boo! Be like that then Mya but I promise you this one thing you will be begging me way before I beg you! Is that right Sebastian? Well I got a surprise for you I walked to the room and got my dildo it's got eight different speeds on it and he has not seen this one. I walked pass the living room into the kitchen I got the bottle of champagne and two glasses with everything in tow I head back to the living room where Sebastian is stroking his dick nice and slow I put the glasses on the table and lick my lips at him I bend even lower with my ass in the air when I place the champagne down.

Bend over let me see sexy Sebastian holler! So, you want a drink baby? Sure, Mya pour me a little something! Ok I said I gave him his drink we, toast and I swallowed my drink. Take it easy Mya don't get fucked up too fast you might submit! Really Sebastian I do not think so but keep wishing that's all you can do I can't take that away from you! Oh, you funny huh Sebastian says, I said no but I want to show you something, so I got on my knees in front of him facing the TV.

I put my chest on the carpet ass up in the air reaching for my toy I turn it on Sebastian kept saying what are you doing Mya you going to make me fall inside of you the way you bent over like that. I look up at the movie and the sex scenes are hot the guy got her bent over touching her toes while he fucks he in the shower. Sliding the dildo from my clit to my ass so he can see I move slowly up and down the lining of my sex to my ass.

Mya fuck the game I am coming in that pussy if you don't behave, I said I feel naughty baby and I don't to submit at least not today! I turned around to face him my back on the floor and my knees in the air I say you like my come fuck me shoes baby? Yes, Mya he replies and what about my sexy lingerie? Moaning loud Sebastian say fuck baby I love all of it you look so edible and fuck-able right now let me have the pussy come on stop playing Mya!

Fuck-able I like that baby now watch me, turning up the speed I insert my battery operated boyfriend in me I slide it in and out while licking my tongue and moaning I have one hand feeling up my tits as I fuck the toy. I am looking at Sebastian and his eyes are dead in between my thighs I open my legs, wide so he can see me as I ride this dildo. Mya, you can't do this to me baby as he gets off the chair and on to the floor I started scooting back as he got closer he reached for my hand and pulling the dildo out of my hand he slid on top on me and inside me all in one movement.

I raise my ass off the floo,r so he can slide in I whisper yeah baby give me that Rock-Hard dick I think that move you made is called submit but, I love it and Yes, I will submit to you baby I can't resist you for long! Mya, I will submit anytime to you because I see nobody else but you and no one ever satisfy me and my cravings like you do! My dick just wants more and more of you. Sebastian pumped harder and harder, shit I am going to get carpet burns on my back and my ass if I don't watch it. It felt so good I could not stop him I wrap my legs around him as he go hard in the pussy the sweat and moans I put it back on him as he was giving it to me fuck that shit I said flip over baby I want to ride this dick right now.

In the back of my mind I am thinking bitch do what you got to do to get your ass off this floor before you really be out of work for the rest of the week fucking with Sebastian ass! He laid on his back and I got on top facing his legs and sitting on his dick I rocked forward leaned down holding his ankles with my ass in the air I started popping that ass up and down, Sebastian hands on my ass cheeks opening them up and pulling me down all you can hear is the slapping sound. Damn Mya it's never a dull moment with you and I love it so much I am about to cum inside baby you ready for me sexy? Yes, Sebastian I replied then give me all that ass Mame!

Moving faster I tighten up and get ready for him he slapped my ass hard three times then climax oh yeah he, growls my fucking wife I love you baby till death do us part only I hope I don't have to beat your ass before natural causes kick in. You better not give my loving away to no one man or woman you hear me Mya? Yes, Sebastian I hear you loud and clear you could have at least waited until we got married to be threatening my life, damn I look forward to coming home to your aggressive ass every day! He slaps my ass get up baby let me wash you off. OH, now you want to wash me off? Just a minute ago you were going to beat my ass make up your mind crazy man! Sebastian ran water in the tub for our bath I want to ask him about the ring because I am anxious to know but I decided to leave it alone I don't want to ruin the moment for him we slip in the tub on opposite sides my feet on his chest he rubbed my feet and I rubbed his. the water felt so good and relaxing Sebastian said so you let Gisele eat you, wow I can't believe you took that chance at work Mya that really concerns me!

I said baby let's leave that alone please that was a bad judgment call on my part I should have known better. Trust me I have beaten myself up over it going forward I am for certain that I would not make such a dumbass decision again. I, know for sure that I don't want to lose you and what we have Sebastian certainly not over a slight lack of common sense. So, let me ask you something Mya what are you going to do when you see her at work? I said well the good thing is we don't work in the same office and we are on different floors I am not going to stress myself over it I am just going to be cordial to her that's it. You better hope this shit doesn't get out remember people love gossip especially office gossip! Sebastian, I said exasperated did not do anything to her she ate me so why would she tell anybody anything? I don't know Mya but now you are knee deep in the shit. I sigh I am exhausted baby I am going to go lay down I got too much on my mind right now. Sebastian says no you don't get away that easy this is the consequences of you fucking actions so don't run away face it you made a fucked up, decision and now you should figure out how you going to deal with this at work you can't call off every day Mya. Damn Sebastian I know and guess what you are pissing me off let's flip the switch and talk about your encounter with your ex-girlfriend. NO, we fucking will not flip the switch Mya because I don't live in the same state with her and I don't work with her and that was so fucking long ago your shit is recent I don't want to have to worry about every time you take your ass to work you maybe in an awkward position with Gisele it's obvious she knows how to get the you and you were weak for her what makes you think she would not try again Mya? I said shit I should have gone to work today if I only knew this is how things would have been. Well it's too late now Mya you are here, and these are things we need to discuss we are engage, to be married and sometimes we are going to have to face the tough situations we must communicate that way when we walk away everything is understood and neither of us is left wondering.

We should be secure in our relationship so let's work the kinks out now, so we can walk down that isle in peace. The tears started rolling down my eyes I just shook my head ok I was trying to get out the tub when Sebastian reached over to wipe my tears he said I know it's difficult to discuss but I don't want to hold this against you we both made mistakes and we both fessed up to it my love for you have not changed a bit baby I want you to know that you are beautiful. And I don't blame Gisele for trying to holla at you baby you're very sexy and beautiful you cannot take risks like that you understand what I am saying Mya? I could not stop the tears from running down my face all I could get out of my mouth was I am so sorry baby it would not happen again I promise you if things get too difficult to bear I would find another job I would do whatever it takes because I don't want you to worry that I will slip up again. In my mind.

I am thinking how the fuck did I end up in the hot seat wow I must get out this tub I just want to lay down. I reached over to Sebastian and leaned in to kiss him my hands caressing his face I said baby I am getting out of the bath I want to go lay down. But before I go I wanted to say thank you for loving me, I truly love you! We both got out the tub I dried up and laid on the bed I am physically and emotionally exhausted I need rest. Lay down baby I will lotion you up what do you want to wear? Sebastian said I replied boy shorts and wife beater he laughed!

I just want to be comfortable right now and getting lotion down and dressed my fiancé is A bonus that I will love. Well it's all part of loving you Mrs. Gutierrez now lay your ass down and let me rub you down. I giggled as he began to lotion my body Sebastian massage my shoulders all the way down to my feet he slide my panties on me and after kissing each nipple I sit up so he can put my t-shirt on he lays me down gently I pull him so he can lay with me he wrapped his hands around me as I bury my face in his chest and snuggle in to sleep Sebastian stroke my hair as I move my hand up and down his back.

I sigh hmmm fighting sleep then I gave in we slept for about three hours by the time I woke up we both were on other ends of the bed. I stayed still for a minute then Sebastian rolls over I whisper baby I am going to get up and cook something for us to eat! He replied ok baby and gave me the softest kiss in the world it felt a bolt of electricity that went instantly to my vagina all I can say was ooh baby we kissed over and over again I rolled on top of Sebastian touching his face as I kiss him back feeling his arms wrapped around me caressing my back, I grind on his growing penis slowly, I started moaning as we kissed Sebastian grinding back on me I whispered in his ear baby you know I can cum like this! OH, yeah Mya let me help you cupping my ass started pulling me into him as we grind harder boning sliding up and down on each other I can feel my clit pulsating.

I reach over to kiss his neck licking his neck back to his lips we suck each other tongue passionately hmm I murmur I started to move faster up and down his dick my panties leaking they are soaking wet and I about to cum I can feel I spread my legs a little wider so his dick can have better access to my clit oh baby I moaned I am Cumin oh yes baby my legs were trembling Sebastian rips the panties off and pulled off his boxers I stuck his dick inside of me I laid on his chest and he work his hands on my ass pushing me up and down Sebastian whisper lay here on me baby I want to feel your body on my body Mya oh yeah baby just like that push back on my dick baby you feel like you flooded down there you so wet damn baby kiss my neck for me he says!

I smiled and kissed his neck and nibble off his ear lobe as I whisper your dick is so hard baby I feel it inside of me pushing back on him I can feel it building up for me to cum again I said can I wet you baby I want to wet you Sebastian, can I? Wet me down Mya yes that what I need to feel this went cunt oh fuck Mya come baby gimme all you got for some more dick sexy! I came panting and kissing him, he slaps my ass I can feel his dick rock hard damn baby I said wow you are swollen right now I love it. Sebastian slaps my ass again growling come baby gimme that pussy it's mines, right? He slaps my ass again as he repeated his self I screamed yes at the same time he slapped my ass again. Wet my dick one more time before I cum Mya he growls I need that right now I said bite my neck baby and I will cum.

I move my neck by his lips he bit into my neck and my pussy responded I moaned as he bite me I said harder baby I moaned right there baby right there he slapped my ass and I came; my legs we about to give way they were shaking.

Sebastian let out a big growl damn baby I am about to release inside of you I sat up on and rode his dick I had on hand pulling my nipples and the other playing with my clit so he can see his hands on my hips pulling me down harder I take all him he is solid hard from the love faces he is making and the way he is growling I know that he is about to explode.

I let him take the lead I said get it like you like it baby I can feel his body move under me looking at him I felt a surge of electricity he me I moan oh baby we are staring each other in the eye it's so intense he growls and I moan deeply oh baby take it, it's all your Sebastian take it baby I screamed as he pulls me down really hard again and again I am going to wet, you down I said he slapped my ass hard I came then he came all his muscles tense in his body he kept pumping until he got all of it out I collapse on his chest and lay there for few minutes until I can catch my breath.

Sexy 9

When we both calm down I said ok I am going to take a quick shower then I will cook something for us to eat. I slide off him and hit the showers thinking about what to cook I shake my head got out the shower and threw on my robe I said honey what do you feel like eating he said just do something simple baby I am going to jump in the shower right now.

I said ok that still does not say what you want to eat can you be a little more specific please? Sebastian said I don't know baby whatever you make is fine with me didn't we have food from dinner last night warm that up! I said Yeah, I forgot about that ok that's what's up so food would be ready when you get out of the shower. I throw on one of Sebastian t-shirt with no panties because I am sore it needs to air out I warm up the food set the table we ate quietly both of us was hungry after eating I cleaned up the place change sheets while Sebastian did the dishes and mop the kitchen floor we relaxed him in his recliner and I laid on the couch I got the laptop and searched for wedding dresses.

Sebastian watched soccer and the phone rings, it's my Mom I answer hi Mom she said I have been calling you at work are you okay I said Mom call my cell phone if you need me I always have my cell on me even in meetings and I will get back to you when I am available! So what's going on are you ok? Yes, Mya I am fine I was just calling to see if you talked with your sister? I said I will give her a call later right now Sebastian and I are busy so if there is nothing else I will call you back Ma! Just call your sister yall need to get over this nonsense I will not tolerate this crap between you and your sister, so call her and you have a niece that loves you I am sure she will be happy to hear from you Mya. Ok Mom I will, enjoy the rest of your day my fiancé is calling me bye Ma! I hung up the phone quickly before she could say anything. Sebastian was just looking at me and shaking his head I looked at him and roll my eyes, he said you know you wrong from hanging up so quickly! Sebastian, I did tell her we were busy now I know she is not going to call back. I would like to enjoy the rest of my evening drama free if you don't mind we have enough going on in our home I need to stay focus on us it's important to me baby.

Mya, I understand what you are saying but at some point, you should inform everyone the right way of our engagement this might back fire on you now that you mentioned it to your Mom I am sure she is calling everyone she knows to tell them, don't be surprise if your phone starts to ring off the hook so say goodbye to peace and quiet. Quickly I said bullshit I got the ringer on silent honey I am not available for comments. I went back to looking at dresses for my wedding day I seriously just want to keep my mind clear and free. I don't even want to think about work at all. Sebastian asks what am I doing I said looking at ideas for our wedding he said I don't care what you do just make sure we have a live band. Sure, that's fine I do want to keep nice and small I rather spend money on a nice honey moon you know it's not about everybody it about us. I would family and close friends to celebrate with us, but I want our new beginning to be perfect.

I guess I will be trying to get at least an hour per day overtime. Yeah, I know I need to work some overtime too Sebastian said I would love for us to go on a beach with white sands I would love to do a day of sailing especially in the evening watching the sun go down that will be so romantic you know babes. I said yes, I would love that too oh just getting up in the morning checking out local markets and then sailing and drinking champagne that will be so beautiful ok baby let me search south of France packages but what is our time frame to get married?

Sebastian replied at least in the next six months that will give us some time to save for the trip and pull the wedding off let's talk to the pastor this Sunday at church once to tie down a date we can go from there maybe keep the reception at the hotel my brother works at that way we can get a good discount if we can save there we can definitely go to South of France and we need at least a week down so figure out a date remember I have to give advance notice to the job Mya. I know Sebastian I have to do the same thing I must give notice six months from now we are looking at a Christmas or New Year's Day wedding!

Mya wait a minute that may not be such a bad idea lets have the wedding on New Year's Day after service we can flow into our wedding ceremony keep it short and sweet then celebrate with family and friends they all go to church on New Year's anyway so this will be an extra special one for all of us! That sounds great ok well we should get to church on Sunday for sure ok let me see I started typing packages for France I am started to get excited I said with a big smile on my face.

Sebastian looked at me as our eyes met we both chuckled I said yes baby we finally doing it I am so happy right now I got up off the couch and give him a kiss a sweet kiss no dramatics just gentle enough to let him know I love him but aggressive enough, so he knows I am for real. Sitting on the couch I began my search I hope we can afford these packages especially around that time people travel so we should consider holiday travel to baby. I said, Sebastian put his head back on the chair and said well lets at least see what the numbers look like and decided from there if anything we can do the justice of the peace with immediate family and then throw a get together in your mothers back yard.

I said hell fucking no I want to walk down the aisle buddy so if you want to have a reception in the alley I don't care but we will get married in the church I will walk down the aisle and that's all I really look forward to we can go to a burger joint for our reception for all I care I don't give two flying seven forty- seven, fuck and that's the gospel according to NAS. Damn Mya calm your ass down I was just making, a suggestion! I'm trying ok? to look for ways to cut cost the more we save the more we can spend on us, right? Ok Sebastian I agree but I will give you the live band if you give me the church wedding anything else we can compromise on agreed? Yes, Mya agreed ok let's move on what kind of numbers are you seeing for flight and hotel also check out newlywed packaged we might get a discount there I see a Thirty- five hundred dollars honeymoon suite this includes air and hotel in France this is an elite hotel though that's why it's a little expensive. I will keep searching. SO, what theme are we going to have for the reception and what colors I asked? Listen Mya the theme is wedding nothing else no crazy shit nothing like that l just want it to be simple.

Sebastian we still need to have a theme like a traditional wedding or since we are having a New Year wedding we can do like a winter wonderland theme everything white with icicles and snowflakes decoration with blue lighting oh baby that will be beautiful I am really getting excited so that's the theme what do you think. Well Mya its sounds beautiful I guess I am going to have to find me a part time job to be able to pull this off see looking at you and seeing your eyes light upI want you to have the wedding of your dreams.

Oh baby I can start back working part time at the gym that

will keep me in shape and it will earn us extra money. We probably would have to cook more and stop eating out as much as we do that will save so money. I know right Sebastian mutters Yeah, we must find ways to cut cost maybe we should stop fucking so much that might save on the water bill you know them long baths and washing sheets. Ha -Ha Sebastian I don't think so no sex is not an option now you trying to be funny.

Mya if you can keep your drawers on we can say money Sebastian says with a smirk on his face. I mean baby I am just saying you don't give my dick a chance to breathe Richard needs his rest. Ah Ok keep talking shit and see how that turns out for you I told you before if I close shop hmm you going to need a jack hammer to pry that bitch open Mr. Gutierrez.

Mya don't tempt me sweet heart you and I know I will always get what I want when I what it you can't resist me, and I have some tricks up my sleeve I have not pulled out yet either way I will get the pussy dry or wet your choice it's you that's going to swollen. I will be ok please believe me sugar pie Sebastian says laughing. I shake my head I am going into the bedroom you are ruining my concentration

Sebastian.

Ok bye Mya shit finally I can watch the game! Just for that comment Sebastian I should stay just to annoy you, but I am not in the mood so watch your game. As I pass by Sebastian I reached over and whisper in his ear, and by the way honey the shop is closed the building is foreclosed you going to have to pay a hefty fine to reopen the shop that is if I let you. Challenge is on smart ass! Sebastian said shit I ain't worried about it do what you should do, and I am going to do the same.

I hope you don't eat them words sweet heart. Now shew fly don't bother me. Sebastian made a hand gesture as he shewed me away. Like shew fly don't bother me. I rolled my eyes at him I really want to slap him in the back of his head, but I held back my twitching palm and walked into the bedroom and shut the door hard. I can hear Sebastian laughing out loud in the living room I refuse to get uptight, so I shrug it off myself. it's all in good fun anyway and may the best man or woman win.

Good luck buddy I hollered out to him and he responds good luck to you sexy! I decided to call my best friend Tamia to see how she is doing the phone rings she answered on the first ring she says girl you going to live long I was just about to call you I said oh what is going on T you alright yes Mya I am doing fine Tyler little butt got into a fight in school I just took everything from him play station XBOX, his phone you name it,I just had to shut his ass down. Wow Tamia what was he fighting for? Mya please this fool was fighting over a little girl I want to kick his ass right now, but I figure if I take everything from him it will hurt him more. Shit I flip through his phone and apparently, he and that hefer have been sexting.

Tamia shut up! I said what, how old is he again? Thirteen with a bad attitude! Well if I know one thing about you Tamia you going to deal with his ass right and how is Reggie doing he still in the picture I asked. Hmm let me tell you all the men in my life are acting the plum fool and Reggie just made the list he had me waiting up for him last night we were supposed to go to movie, he never showed and never called and when I called his phone went straight to voice mail. I just need a vacation from all they asses Mya.

I know that's right Tamia well maybe you can come up for a weekend I need help planning the wedding! The wedding Mya what did Sebastian propose? Yes, girlfriend that is why

I was calling you I want to tell you the good news. Oh, Mya congratulations I am so sorry you called me and here I am running my mouth about my problems, Mya I am so happy for you and excited of course I am going to come and spend a weekend with you I would love to help you plan. Cool I am so happy right now Tamia and I told him about Gisele we went through the motions, but this was after he ask me to marry him yesterday I took the day off today because we were too tired after last night dinner and love making.

What did he say when you told him about Gisele she asked. He said he cannot believe that I would jeopardize my job and basically, he is worried it may happen again, but I know who I want you know? Yes, Mya I know! And Tamia I am so for sure that I don't want to be in this life without Sebastian by my side I mean he gives me everything I ever need and want the experiment is over been there done that now on to my new life. I am so happy for you and it is well deserve and is about time you have some kids in your life. Whatever Tamia I maybe already Prego the way we have been sexing lately I am in the bedroom trying to get some space the damn pussy is officially dead and swollen I got to let her rest I said laughing. Tamia started to laugh loudly she said I am so glad you called Mya you made my day ok let me

146

work out a good time and I will make plans to come spend time with you.

Thank you, Tamia well call me if you need to talk I am going to surf the web for some ideas we will talk later. Yes, we will Mya we will soon! Ok thank you enjoy the rest of the day the best you can go take a long bath with some candles oh and yes have a glass of wine or better yet a shot of tequila. Tamia giggles yes tequila sounds better than wine right now ok my dear you take care, love you Mya. I said I love you Tamia later! We hung up and I rolled back in the bed and close my eyes I am getting married wow who knew my mom words would make such an impact on my life and my fiancé is the man of my dreams my mind was everywhere I cannot believe it I want my wedding to be nice and beautiful not boring so many thoughts so many ideas.

And even though I am happy and excited I am starting to feel a little bit overwhelmed and I should stop drinking asap just in case I am in fact pregnant I should take a test I jumped out the bed I called Sebastian as I got into the living room he was getting up from the chair to come and see what I wanted. What's wrong baby he asked I said I need to go get tested and I must stop the drinking we have been fucking like minks I want to make sure you know?

Damn Mya I did not even think about that yes you are right we need to make sure go get dress lets go to the drug store and buy a test we can check ourselves then you need to make an appointment with your doctor as soon as possible. I said ok let's go we got dressed and suddenly, I feel nervous because I have been drinking I don't want to be pregnant right now I want to get the wedding over with and get myself alcohol free that way I can have a healthy baby.

I looked at Sebastian all worried he cupped my face with his hand looking deep in my eyes he said don't panic baby let's find what is going on first we may not have anything to worry about as he kissed my forehead the tears are running down my eyes damn baby I have been so damn emotional lately right now I feel scared as hell oh I pray that I am ok.

You are ok Mya come on get the car it felt like forever to get to the pharmacy my heart is beating fast wow Sebastian I am nervous I said breaking the silence he reassured me that we will be ok. We arrive and walk in Sebastian hands around my waist we walked to the pharmacist and ask which product is reliable and can detect early pregnancy. The pharmacist said the absolute best test is a blood test it can detect it early and then he handed us a product we can use at home we bought two and head home on the way home Sebastian asked if I wanted to stop and get something to eat I said I am not hungry at all I just want to go home. Mya just relax and stay calm we are almost home.

Ok baby let me read the instructions in the meantime it says if the line turns a pink color its positive. Well lets go find out Mya come on we get back in the house and Sebastian follows me to the bathroom; he opened the package and I sat down did the test and then we waited for the results which seemed like an eternity I walked to the kitchen and got a glass a water and came back not change I felt relief and disappointed at the same time Sebastian said well according to this we are not pregnant but I want you to make that appointment with your doctor I said yes I will baby but right now I am feeling my appetite is coming back let's get something to eat.

Let's get some stew fish and dumplings from up the road and come home I want to relax its back to work tomorrow and I am sure I have a lot of work to do. Okay Mya lets go I agree I want to relax also let's go to bed early tonight I just want to hold you and feel your heartbeat as I sleep. Oh, baby you know how to make me smile I would love you to hold me close Sebastian I really love you baby I really do.

He reached over and kissed me so soft I can feel my body melt in his arms. His lips so soft on mines I breathe and take his scent into my senses hmm I murmur holding him closer I cherish these moments this is the part when my heart skips a beat and I know like I know that I love this man he is my life. Sebastian stopped and looked at me and whispers yes tell me? Without hesitation I said you are my life I know you are the one for me! as I looked in his eyes a tear formed in my eyes and in his. Mya don't cry baby you break my heart when you cry I love you more that you know and I cannot see my life without you we will be alright.

Now come on let's get out of here and get something to eat before we start eating each other I laughed and slip on my shoes, hand in hand we walked to the corner to get our food. I ordered stew fish with cornmeal dumplings, sweet potatoes, plantains and cassava also please put extra sauce on it and some pepper please. Sebastian looked at me and said damn Mya you must be eating for two because I've never seen you eat or order in that combination. Sebastian what are you ordering while you all up in my food? He smirked and said give me a chicken roti with plenty pepper. I laughed and shake my head and you talking about me baby look at you. What you know about roti your parents from Mexico City! Mya it's just like a burrito. No Sebastian it's similar but not the same but ok I want to see this, and you better eat all of it too while you are asking for plenty pepper.

We both laugh even the clerk was laughing we paid and sat while waiting for the food Lisa called I answered and she said I have to talk to you can we meet somewhere I said sure, but I am getting ready to eat so can let's do tomorrow lunch at my office. Sebastian kept looking at me intently I said okay Lisa I will see you tomorrow honey say hi to your brother before he has a damn heart failure please. I gave him the phone and rolled my eyes! The clerk waved to me to get the food by the time I came back to the table Sebastian was hanging up the phone. Let's go baby I motioned to him, so what's up with Lisa he asked I said we just meeting for lunch some girl talk we don't get together as often as we should, and she is family now I might as well spend some time with her. I like that Mya that makes me feel good to know you all get along I must talk to you Mom you know!

Talk to my Mom I said Yes Mya I should ask for your permission to marry her daughter so maybe this weekend we can have dinner I will call my dad tonight. Ok Sebastian I will organize something for us that will be nice I can't wait to get in the house I am ready to eat we should have taken a few bites while we were there. I feel Mya but once we eat we can lay down and get some much- needed rest which reminds me I need to call Ricardo and see what went on at work today. My heart jumped in my throat I manage to mutter ah ok baby. I am thinking boy if only you knew what Ricardo been up to you will be going crazy right about now, keeping my cool we go in I immediately start eating at the table I waived at Sebastian don't talk to me right now because I am not going to answer look on my face he raised his top lip to the side and roll his eyes in the back of his head.

The food taste so good hmm Sebastian and I ate in silence and I enjoyed it.   My mind drifted on the work day, tomorrow but I quieted the thought embracing the peace is all I wanted and so did my stomach. Yawning I said oh baby I full I am going to take a quick shower then later down see you when you get in bed. Mya, it is not even seven o clock we can chill for a while! Sebastian, I said you can chill if you want I have had an emotional and what seems like a long weekend I just want to lay in my clean sheets and relax even if I am not at sleep. Come on Mya why you acting like this? Come on Sebastian I need some rest so stay up with you want baby I am out smooches! Yeah ok Sebastian said smooches baby go rest.

I took a short shower and slipped in the bed my intentions were to pick out what I am going to wear to work tomorrow that way I don't have to be looking. That idea went out of my head as soon as I hit the pillows after repeatedly yawning my body give in and I fell asleep before I knew it was ten o clock when Sebastian slipped in the bed he pushed me to my side, I looked at the time pulled him close matching his breathing I fell asleep thinking here is where I always want to be. I woke up to a hard dick on my back the alarm went off I have thirty more minutes before I get off the bed I hit the alarm and attempted to go back to sleep when I feel Sebastian hands between my legs I said oh no I have to work baby!

You went to bed early baby Sebastian said now my dick is rock hard and I need to feel that tightness just stay still I want it from behind. Hmm no I had thirty minutes now it's about twenty- five minutes before I go to work Mr. Gutierrez. By this time Sebastian was already inside of me; I close my eyes, I chuckled and said I guess you just going to take it huh! You right about that Mrs. Gutierrez I practically own the pussy now.

Sebastian said in a raspy deep voice. It felt good, but I refuse to make a sound then he hit it hard I gasp. Yes! Mya that's is what I want to hear you I told you I need my pussy coherent, I smiled and said whatever baby just hurry up before the alarm goes off again. Just stay your ass still Mya I got this you will be freshly fucked in a minute then you can go make daddy his money. Whatever Sebastian your ass is fucking crazy I said laughing. My breathing got heavier as the strokes go in an out I want call out his name fuck it I just gave in as the moans got louder so did daddy his long strokes got shorter and harder.

Oh, get it baby I muttered and my juices flowed Sebastian whispers yes Mya baby wet me down just like that!

Sexy 10

Feeling the warmth of his breath on my neck with his soft kisses and hearing his voice my body started to tremble as I feel his dick get rock hard in the pussy I tighten my muscles, closed my eyes and let the moment take me I am high on ecstasy I feel myself about to explode I my movement matches his I screamed baby I am about to cum his fingers moved around my clit his strokes got harder I feel like I am going crazy, my panting got louder oh daddy I screamed oh baby I can feel you Sebastian whispers ah ha so come for daddy baby girl.

At his command I exploded my legs are shaking my body felt weak as Sebastian kept pumping his dick in me I came again. Damn baby Sebastian gimme on me one more sexy release them juices one more time and let daddy cum. Oh fuck daddy bite my neck and I am going to cum I move my head a little so he can bite my neck on the second bite I came and Sebastian growled I am Cumin Mame the electricity ran through us it was so crazy tears started to roll down my eyes.

As we calmed down I whisper to Sebastian no one has ever sexed me to tears. Mya that's what you get with Premium Grade A type dick! I tried to get out of his hold, but he held me tighter. Let me go Sebastian I have to get, dress for work plus you made me mad.

Mya, you know I am just kidding I felt the energy too and I love when I feel that way and I love you so get your freshly fucked ass in the shower and go make my money woman I got a ring to buy I can't get it with you slacking off Sebastian said with a grin I threw a pillow at his and said whatever you go make my blasted money! With that said I ran into the shower I've got to figure out what I am wearing for work today shit last night I was too tired to look for anything.

I hollered at Sebastian to put the TV on and check the temperature. That way I know what to put on. As the water run down my face, I smiled to myself and thought damn I am really, happy and engage who knew this would all happen this weekend; had so much up and downs but we made it through and all I can do is not to dwell on the past but focus on the future. I have a wedding to plan whoo hooo! I did not realize I said that loud until I heard

Sebastian yell be quiet you will wake up the neighbors I said fuck the neighbors I am happy.

I got out, got dressed kissed my fiancé goodbye and head into the jungle to work as I walked in the building I say Gisele I said hello and kept it moving she seem to be in shock but the look on my face was like I don't give a fuck don't speak to me right now. I did not even get on the elevator I went to get a white chocolate mocha from the café shop on the lower level then I went up to the office good morning Mr. Jordan I said as I pass by his office.

How are you feeling Mya I said I feel a lot better than I did yesterday Mr. Jordan so what is the priority list today. He said let's have a meeting in fifteen minutes once you settle in Mya. Ok I responded I check my messages while taking a few sips of my mocha. I buzzed Mr. Jordan to see if he ready he said yes so with my note pad I head into his office. As I walked in, my conscious got a hold of me oh shit Friday with Gisele I hope no one heard us! I sat down flipping the pages in my note book for a clean page. There seem to be an issue, with their quarterly statements scan them for any discrepancies and we can meet this afternoon. I have a board meeting at nine and we will meet later. I said ok so how was everything yesterday. Everything went well Mya I had a couple of emails what saved was the email you sent me Friday with my schedule for the beginning of the week that helped me a lot and the files you organized, I could find my way.

I want to thank you it really helped a lot! No problem Sir I will send you an email at the end of the day, so you have a heads up for the next day tasks, I am glad it helped I was a little worried there! Thanks again Mya, ok I've forwarded you some emails please respond to the inquiries and cc me on the critical ones only.

Ok Sir is that it? Yes, Mya by the way is everything ok with you, you have been ill a lot lately I said yes Sir I am just having some stomach issues, but I am fine. Ok Mya well welcome back I heard everything was quite on Friday? Yes, Sir it was! I replied looking for some indication on his face that he heard through office gossip that Gisele was in my office with the door close for about thirty minutes or so shit I can't remember the time, but my nerves is kicking in and my heart is racing.

But nothing so shifting my thoughts I asked Sir is it ok for me to work an extra hour a day to catch up on work since I was off yesterday I have the Isaac Inc file to set up and because of the time difference I may have to come in a little early to catch them in the office since they are overseas. Sure, Mya I don't have a problem with that go for it! Ok we will meet later thank you Sir! I went back to my office I need to do some re-organizing, I buzzed Mr. Jordan oh by the way I am ordering supplies today Sir please email me your list if you can before your meeting. Sure, Mya he responded! Moving on I am trying to keep my mind clear of any distractions and get back into work mode hmm let me pull the files he needs and scan them, so I can move on with my other tasks.

As I pulled the files my phone rings I answered Mr. Jordan's Office Mya speaking how can I help you and it was Sebastian Hey lover he said, I replied hey you! What's up? I just called to say I love you sexy see you tonight and have a good day Mya. Right back at you Sebastian I said smiling from ear to ear see you late baby bye and we hung up. I continued scanning through the files and it just dawn on me I should call Lisa I have a lunch date with her today I hope everything is ok she should have the result of the pregnancy test oh man I hope things isn't as ugly as I think, I text her to see if we were going to still meet. I got a quick response yes Mya I will call you when I am close I responded ok Sister in Law see you then. Lisa replied with a smiley face. Smiling to myself I thought see it just the little things that count! Back to the files I made notes of a couple of things that stood out to me clearly there have been some changes in the expenses and overtime which could be a reason for question.

I started to respond to some of the emails just to take my eyes off the files I will re-visit them again with fresh eyes just to make sure nothing was overlooked. My phone rings again but I noticed the number its Gisele shit I am not answering that phone call at all. I let it go to voice mail, what the hell does she want? It is what it was, like that shit was so yesterday thank you for everything but so much has changed since our encounter but I don't owe you an explanation so go away you met my man, so you know what it is play you position chick! I had to calm my mind down I was on a roll there falling back into work answering a few emails and returning calls took up most of the morning which I appreciate; it kept me focus and now it's time for lunch with Lisa.

I text here to meet me at the taco spot two blocks away they have tables outside and it's such a nice day! I spotted Lisa walking down the block I waived to her as we got closer I reached out and gave her a much -needed hug. So, what's going on Lisa? Well Mya I am pregnant, and it is for Ricardo according to the due date I am so scared I don't know what to tell Josh I have not been letting him touch me and what's worst I cannot stop thinking of Ricardo he takes my body places I've never been. Mya, I don't know what to do and then my brother let's not talk about him. Calm down Lisa just take a deep breath you are doing too much right now you need to slow your roll, you are heading downhill fast so calm down. Ok so the baby is Ricardo's did you tell him yet? Yes, I told him, and he wants me to leave Josh and move in with him right away!

But I can't I don't want to hurt Josh, but I don't love him the way I used to anymore I feel like everything is so routine in our relationship I want to feel excited and Ricardo does that for me. Lisa either way you look at it you will be hurting Josh because if you stay and lie about the baby being his when it's not at some point the truth will come out. And if you leave his feelings will be hurt but he will get over it rather than getting over a child that is not his. So, think about it and make the right decision even ask Ricardo questions to make sure he will handle his business. I don't suggest you move in with anyone maybe you should be on your own for a while just to figure things out because jumping from relationship to another does not give you time to heal no matter how you feel about Ricardo take your time to know him as far as your brother goes we just got engaged the wedding will keep him busy tell him when the time is right this is after all your life dear; live to the best of your ability.

I said to Lisa by this time the tears were running I said suck it up honey you let Ricardo put the smack down on your ass now you are paying the price, but big girls don't fall we stand tall so dry them tears up and start living. Anyway, Lisa I must go so let's catch up later this week, I said to Lisa as she dries her eyes she responded sure I should get back myself, thank you so much Mya I will call you later. I gave her a big hug and left, I know that I really did not help her much, but I wanted this decision to be something she made on her own. Back to work the evening when quickly I had a meeting with Mr. Jordan then I headed home I was happy to get in the house my baby is cooking I walked up and kiss him grabbing his ass I whisper hi honey how was your day? Sebastian answered it was good and yours? I said it was good uneventful it smells good in here honey what are you cooking?

You will see once you freshen up for evening dinner! Sebastian said in an English accent which made me giggle. I walked off to the bedroom to take a shower hmm I should surprise my man he is making dinner and I am going to heat up the room. I started searching my closet oh where did I put the sexy negligée? The one that's floor length with the slit up each side and my Cinderella glass heals! Yes, okay let me shower I thought to myself oh this is going to be good I am excited.

Pulling my hair up into a ponytail I slip out of my work clothes and into the shower I had to jump back for a second because the water was so hot! I could not stop smiling while thinking of how I am going to reward Sebastian for being so thoughtful. After a through wash I lotion up, spray some perfume and slip on my negligée no panties of course I finish the outfit with a matching robe. Some light powder on my face with the cranberry color lipstick my heals. I leave my hair up and I text Sebastian to ask him if dinner is ready?

He responded yes get your ass in here woman. I text him

back I'll be right their honey! Strutting my stuff, I walked over to the dining table where Sebastian stood. Madam he waived to me as I got closer he took me into his senses lightly kissing my neck I can hear his breathing hmm you smell delicious sexy! I smiled and replied thank you Mr. Gutierrez. Sitting down Sebastian adjusts my chair, I said the food looks great I can't want to eat so come on and sit and with me. Patients my dear Mya let me get us some drinks! Finally, Sebastian sat down he is such a perfectionist we blessed the food and ate everything taste so good baby thank you! I said as I took another bite I can see a smile creeping out of the corners of his lips. My pleasure Mrs. Gutierrez and you look beautiful tonight! Anything for you my love I whispered I held my glass up for a toast to us and to happiness. I leaned over the table to give him a kiss I can taste the wine on his lips. The wine is perfect with the spaghetti and ground turkey meat sauce! Sebastian says Yes, I totally agree baby and I'll have to reward you so save some wine for later I want to lick it off you!

Damn Mya you got my dick rock fucking hard right now the way you say things to me drives me crazy! Sebastian baby you should finish your food I slide under the table and unzip his pants damn baby you are about to burst through your pants. Sebastian pushed his chair back away from the table, moving closer to his rock-hard dick I take him in my mouth slowly I can hear Sebastian breathing heavily and calling my name which is turning me on. Keeping a steady motion, I move up and down as I lick the tip before I go all the way down as I come up I can feel him swelling I started sucking with no hands I can feel Sebastian hands in the back of head pulling me up and down the moans are loud I can feel the wetness between my legs, I moaned as I deep throat his dick. He throws his head back while pulling my head up and down I can feel he is about to climax.

Sucking even faster and faster he looks down at me our eyes focus on each other I am breathing heavily with his as I suck faster he whispers you make daddy explode Mame, get it for me come on get it me I can feel the electricity between us I started to scream, Sebastian said stay still baby as he holds my head still he eased his dick in and out my mouth as he whispers suck it baby! suck my dick for me baby! OH, yeah that's right just like as he pushes it in my mouth he tells me to suck him. I about to fucking combust I'm watching him as he fucks my mouth his body started to tense up finally he let it go and came I sucked and swallowed all of him. I kept sucking until I got all of him pulling me up Sebastian clear the table told me to lay down my legs were on his legs as he sits down he pulls me down closer pouring some wine between my legs I look up at the ceiling as I feel his tongue lick the wine of my sex. Mya, you are so wet I want you to cum some more let me taste you Cumin. My body went limp, my nipples got hard and my clit was at attention. I sat up on the table so I can watch his tongue go to work I open my legs wide and pull his head in as got close grinding my pussy all in his face he pushes me back down with his hands playing with my nipples and his head between my legs I am out of control all I can do he call his name panting I screamed out oh baby don't stop I love the way you making me feel I sit up just a little so I to lick me I pulled his head in with one hand, grinding harder oh fuck yeah baby I am about to cum on your tongue you got me so fucking hot!

Sebastian grabbed my ass and pulled me so he can access the tip of my clit licking and sucking I'm about to cum baby my legs started to shake I can feel it I stay still pulling his head in with both hands as I lay back I open my legs as wide as I can let him lick and lick as I climax the aftershock made my body shiver. Sebastian finger fucking me and blowing on me I can go again if he started it up again I was thinking to myself I am on fire.

He asks more baby? I said yes please I would love more baby he pours some more wine on me I said wow baby you made me dinner and now you're having me as dessert! Yes, and it's hot and wet just the way I like it Mya. And guess what Mya baby? What I responded I bought you a gift! OH, really let me see Sebastian. No Mya you can feel it though with that said I heard a vibrating sound.

Lay back Mya and stay still Sebastian demanded. I do as I am told but my mind is racing I want to see what it is and how big it is anticipation got me in a panic. Sensing my anxiety Sebastian kisses, me softly between my legs as I began to relax I felt the tip of the vibrator entering me; I moved a little, Sebastian tap my legs to stay still he kept kissing and licking softly as he inserts the toy inside of me. The heat of his tongue with the vibrator cause my juices to start flowing the feeling is indescribable. When I felt I could not take any more Sebastian placed anal beads inside of me that vibrated. Now that caught me off guard I was not prepared for I am being fucked, sucked and butt fucked at the same time all by one man. the movement of this tongue started to increase as my body moves he pulls the anal beads leaving the vibrator going inside of me I stay still every now and then he pulls on the vibrator and push it in.

My body in overload panting loud and moaning I grab my nipples. I am going to explode baby I screamed! Sebastian please baby stop baby he pulled me in close licking my clit I can feel it baby I said I am going to cum baby I put my hands on his head and pull him into my sex letting my juices flow on his tongue. Sebastian moans as I cum he pulled the anal beads intensifying the feeling then he pulled the toy out letting it vibrate on my clit but I can't take any more my body starts to shake I am wounded. Come on Mya lets go to the bedroom I will clean up later. Sebastian picked me up and carried me to the bed he stood over me and said now I know I just satisfy that pussy now I want some ass tonight I want to put the vibrator in your ass one more time before I put my dick in so face down by the foot board and let me do my thing. If it gets to intense baby let know I will stop ok Mya? Ok baby just do your thing! I responded. k Mya you are going to feel something cold baby its only lube then I am going to insert the beads I want you to arch your back for me I want to see that ass hole. Sebastian reaches and lick from my clit to my anus then I feel something cold just relax Mya I got YOU. I am putting the beads in now as he insert, the beads I relax I can feel Sebastian hard dick ease inside of me with short quick jabs he slams into me I screamed oh baby he slams in again I can feel in deep inside of me I wet him down as he hits it again. Yes, Mya let me feel that wetness with another slam he pulled the beads out also pulling his dick from my wet cunt I felt something cold again then slow pushes. My body moved I groaned, Sebastian growled let me get in baby I want this tight ass tonight I am going to go slow I promise baby you speed it up when you are ready.

Slapping my ass Sebastian says come on baby relax! I relaxed and let him in holding my breath I am thinking the shit that women do for their men but if you can't or would not do it I guarantee you that there is someone out there ready and waiting to please your man. With that in mind I suck in the pain and let my man have his way as I relaxed I got into to it pushing back to his grind the noises he made let me know I was pleasing him and he was going crazy I feel his dick pulsating inside of me. I scoot down a little on the bed so he can hit it how he likes.

Oh yeah baby Sebastian growls open that ass for me I grab

hold of the vibrator turning it on I slide it under me I am soaking wet and hot I play with my clit with it, it took my mind off the pain I was feeling Sebastian is at the top of ecstasy his tone is changing his voice is getting deeper as he is about to climax he pulls me in harder and faster I relaxed and let him get it slumping over he cums shaking we both roll to the side laying on the bed I can feel his sweat on my back. In fetal style we cuddle for a minute I am trying to regain strength to get up and take shower, but I decided to lay back and enjoy his arms around me it's what I need right now anyway, I can fall asleep right now I whispered to Sebastian.

He responded go ahead baby pull the cover over us we can just lay here. My heart beat matching his I love this man with all my being right now there is no other place I rather be and would not even take a phone call right now that is how content I am and no one can take this very moment away from me. Sebastian snuggles into me putting his legs over my legs I guess to make sure I don't wonder off anywhere I smiled to myself oh yeah this what I love about my man he makes me feel so secure and in charge. I let myself drift off into a sweet sleep two hours later I feel a nagging pain opening my eyes reluctantly I realize I have to pee shit I don't want to wake Sebastian if I ignore it maybe it will go away temporarily.

But I cannot hold it I must go, I tried to move gently as to not wake him but I failed miserably. Where are you going baby? Sebastian whispers. To the bathroom baby I must pee, sorry to wake you honey but I cannot hold it.

Sebastian tickles me I laugh stop it or I will pee on your ass. I manage to wiggle out of his arms I can feel it coming holding my legs tight I can barely run to the bathroom as I sat down it came down I sigh a sigh of relief that session was so fucking intense I just need to hit the shower more like the tub, but I don't have the strength to wait for the tub to fill up. SO, I run the shower I speak out to ask Sebastian if he is coming in the shower with me. He waves no which is cool with me it's probably better this way anyway that way he does not get any idea. I am enjoying the warmth of the water falling on my face, my shoulders and my back I ended up showering for twenty minutes the room was all fogged up from the heat it smells good in here I dry up and open the door and to my surprise Sebastian is still asleep. I want him to get up so I can change the sheets damn ok off to the living room right now I am being anal retentive and

I know it but after all that sexing I want to sleep in fresh sheets so I make myself some tea and tidy up the kitchen quietly, I pass a mop on the floor and sit down to relax for a second until I go to bed I must make a mental note to call Lisa tomorrow to see how she is doing?

Hmm what should I wear tomorrow if I can find it now I can sleep a little bit later in the morning? Which would be great my ass hurts I need to sleep on my side away from Sebastian and his one hundred percent premium delicious beef dick which I love yep I am sprung here we go T-Pain jamming in my head my thoughts are just ridiculous. Making a mental note of what to wear tomorrow I sigh shit I need to get my ass in the bed I cannot afford to take another day off hmm should I wake him up or just forget it after shutting down the house I head back to the bedroom my baby is sleeping and snoring off to sleep I get on my side and dozed off.

I felt Sebastian move he pulled me into him ah I want to scream because I just shower and oh God no his sweaty ass I am screaming and cussing in my head, but I can't do anything about it I can feel him relax and fall back to sleep. Now there is some shit I can tolerate a funky mofo, ain't it especially when I am fresh and clean. Finally, I relax and give into sleep it seemed like I just laid down when the alarm went off shit I was just sleeping good, too I want to throw the alarm clock out the fucking window right now!

But I don't have the damn strength, so I hit the snooze button Luckily, I have at least three alarms before I get up this first one tells me I have forty minutes to sleep before the next one goes off when that happens it's my warning the last one is get your ass up now or you will be late. Stretching my legs, I roll over and hug my pillow this is my moment to get in so sleep.

I yawn and quickly fall back asleep dreaming I'm walking down the aisle and I see Gisele standing in the front crying I felt so scared I froze in place I can feel my legs tremble, my alarm goes off oh shit I'm trying to open my eyes but I am too deep in so I let the alarm annoy me enough to wake me up I can feel Sebastian wondering hands of hell no pushing his hands away I murmur nope leave me alone I only have a few minutes to sleep so fall back baby. But talking to him ain't, working he kept on fucking with me so I said fuck it and got up shit I need a mental break from my own self and my ever so horny man.

I throw on my robe and walked to the kitchen I need to drink some tea I've got to control my thoughts better I said to myself as I fill the kettle with water I hear Sebastian in the shower hmm what is he doing up as the water heat up I search for the tea bag I made my tea and head to the room. Mya come in here Sebastian says ok baby I replied. Get in the shower babe let me get you washed up to go make my money. I laugh you know you've made that comment before Sebastian! Come on babe you know pimping ain't easy I gotta keep my hoe clean he said laughing.

OH, your ass got jokes this morning huh? If I am your one and only I'll be that hoe, stripper, night nurse and whatever else you want me to be daddy. Hmm is that right Mya? I kind of like this I should get up more often and give you a bath turn now around let me scrub your back for you. I admit this feel so good baby I am sure to have a great day today with the way you are starting my day. He rinsed me off slapping my ass Sebastian says now you are all clean baby go get dressed papa need some brand, new shoes. Yeah ok papa thank you ,for cleaning me up!

As I walked in the room I reached for my tea it's still warm good drinking it down I got dressed. Wow I really feel good our love just seem, to get better Sebastian makes it out of the shower and I walk over and kiss his dick because I can't resist I slide my tongue around it and whisper see you later. You being naughty Mya go make my money! YES, Sir

Pimp Daddy I replied. He smiled your ass is so silly and I love you for it! OH, thank you baby see you later I love, love, love being with you I replied.

Sexy 11

Smiling all the way to work wow this is what true love feels like no boundaries we do what we must do to please each other I truly love this man I am so giddy and high right now and I have not taken any drugs hmm I love this feeling.

The work hours went by quickly I want to surprise my man tonight so I am thinking of a master plan but nothing comes to mind shit I need to check in on my mom I have not spoken to her with Sebastian keeping me hostage and all. Hmm now thinking about there is this sports bar that Sebastian likes to go to he says they have the best wings well I will just text him to meet me there. Immediately the phone rings hi babe I said, Sebastian replied Mya you buying me dinner? I chuckled saying and you know this babe so see you in an hour at the bar. Sebastian gasp and before he could respond I said see you later babe and hung up the phone.

Laughing to myself I rushed home to put on something sexy a tight pair of jeans, come fuck me stilettos and a revealing top sit the girls up with my hot red lipstick yes that ought to get his dick hard. OH, snap I forgot my tightening cream I rushed to the bathroom insert the cream the longer it stays the tighter I should be great! My last touch a spray of Glamorous perfume I feel naughty and sexy I called a cab to the sports bar because I know that Sebastian would want me to ride with him home hmm I feel I slight wet feeling between my legs this damn wayward pussy always at attention and ready to play.

I just love it and I cannot wait to see my baby face the cab pulls up to my destination as I walk in I can see my man at the bar he waves and I put on a sexy smile and strut my stuff over to him I can feel all eyes on me but my eyes were locked on Sebastian sexy ass his eyes light up as I get closer I walked right into his arms gave him a soft kiss on his neck then on his lips hmm Sebastian said you are being naughty tonight and I love it keep it up you might get fucked tonight Mya baby.

I laughed and said well I better keep working in that case, I leaned over and whisper in his ear because the lining of my pussy is already wet for your dick Sebastian baby as I licked his ear I turned around to the bartender and ordered an incredible hulk and an order of hot wings with ranch dressing. Sebastian ordered extra spicy hot wings and two shots of Patron sitting on the bar stool I slide my leg between his. So how was your day Mya he says as his hands moves closer to my inner thighs a wicked smile crosses his face I turned my head and gave him a look out of the corner of my eyes as if to say you better not. The bartender put the drinks down in front of us breaking our stare I quickly reach for my drink trying to move my leg Sebastian give it a squeeze and whispers no leave it here baby needless to say my clit is hard and throbbing shit this Hennessy and Hypnotic has got me feeling a little tipsy.

The wings make it in record time we cheer with a chicken wing before grubbing which forces Mr. man to remove his hands I am happy but sad at the same time I whisper baby we should go fuck in the men's bathroom, with a wolfish grin on his face he replied we can make that happen Mya don't fucking tempt.

Oh daddy I am fucking tempting you please believe it I said while licking my top lip to get the ranch dressing off. Stop Mya consider this your warning if you keep this up all your dreams might come through tonight! Shut up I said as we both burst out laughing, these wings are really, really, good, babe. I think I will order some to go for later tonight. Yeah! know right Sebastian replied so have you spoken to Gisele? Oh, shit where the hell did that come from oh please do not ruin our night with petty bullshit ok come on answer the question bitch you looking guilty right now for no reason at all. I looked in his eyes and simply responded no I have not and I have no intentions of doing so. Sebastian shook his head ok baby I just wanted to make sure she is not trying to steal my woman behind my back you know I hate to have to cut that bitch. Laughing out loud I reached over and kiss his lips saying you don't ever have to worry babe that's not where I want to be I want to be with you I am happy here.

The mood changed Sebastian rubs my face and pulls me in for a sexy kiss that made me groan wow baby I felt giddy I could surrender all right now and I don't give a fuck who his looking my conscious kicks in yeah and you would make the six o clock news you freaky bitch so get a fucking room. Shaking my thoughts off we locked in each other eyes and without words we talk I smile he smile shit this is it for me reality hits I don't want to go nowhere I could not fathom the fucking thought of another woman touching him and that's the way he feels about me so next time my forever horny cunt decides to jump out my drawers to run to Gisele I would scalp that bitch. I shake my thoughts of again damn I have an active imagination. Calm down crazy bitch my conscious rare its ugly head again, fuck off bitch I demand and now I am back on point. Mya do you want another drink and said yes. I do then I want to lick your balls and quite frankly I don't give a fuck if it happens here or in the car. Fuck baby shit you got my fucking dick hard as a mother fucking rock right now. Hey bartender he shouted let me get another shot and an incredible hulk for my hot fiancé.

The bartender replied coming right up! Oh baby order the wings for tonight and let's stop by the liquor store before we go home I said. Damn Mya you trying to get wasted? No Sebastian I want to lick the liquor off your balls if that's alright with you? Hell fucking yeah he responded shit we can go now Mya shit why wait my dick is on twelve o clock and I need to feel them natural juices explode on your tongue the anticipation alone gonna make fucking explode shit so drink up bitch you got dick to suck. I chuckled and said in a very seductive voice oh don't worry fucker you going to be licking to lining of my cunt tonight in exchange for your balls being sucked so don't get fucking cocky.

Hmm I love it when you talk like that Mya so what else you want to do tonight my love your wish is my command that is after you suck my balls make no mistake about that. Laughing I said you got jokes tonight uh? But ok I want to be blind folded and tied up tonight I whisper in his ear I can see the bartender staring at us as my hands travel close to his rock- hard dick on the cool my eyes are roaming the room to see who is paying attention to us as I reach my destination I squeeze gently I can feel it jump in my hand hurry up I am ready to go I demand. Hold on Mya you're getting a little feisty there! I picked up my drink and swallow it down shit I hope my ass can get up and walk out of here, the extra wings came we close our tab and head out as we got to the car it dawned on me I need to go the restroom. Sebastian, I gotta pee so let me put the stuff in the car I am going to go back in since we still here. I will go with you Mya I've seen the way those men were staring at you, ok babe I responded.

We head back into to use the restroom and low and behold there is a family restroom, so Sebastian walks in with me I sit down to pee and as I look up Sebastian is zipping down his pants he pulls out his dick and I open my mouth he knows how much I love to see him with his dick in his hand that shit just turn me on. I lick down the shaft and as promised I began to lick and suck his balls gently the moans coming out of his mouth make me want to climax I am sitting on the toilet drip drying as I suck my fiancé balls. I hear him say in a deep seductive voice I want you to finger fuck yourself Mya I want to see it. Without even thinking I slide my fingers inside my wet cunt and moaned the feeling was so intense. Sebastian moans oh fuck yeah baby his hand sliding up and down his dick as I suck his balls and finger fuck myself.

OH, fuck yeah Mya open your mouth baby and stick your tongue out I am going to jack off in your mouth keep finger fucking that pussy baby don't touch your clit that's for my tongue. As he says that I feel the electricity my moans are becoming deeper the noise from the bar is loud enough to muffle our moans I look up and Sebastian is looking down at me he beats his dick on my tongue every now and then I deep throat it to keep it wet. With one hand on the back of my head Sebastian whispers I am about to cum baby suck me off hard baby.

I quickly oblige as he pulls me in and fucks my mouth I suck hard and make him cum swallowing all every drop of him.

I can feel him getting weak, my hands are now around his waist holding him I can hear him call my name over and over and again and it feels good because I know he is satisfied. Let's get out of here baby I wipe myself wash my hands and he head out and it seems like all eyes were on us we smiled and exited quickly. I want to take you somewhere Mya let's go! I said ok we got in the car and drove to secluded park what are we doing up baby? You will see Mya take your pants off put your heels back on and get out the car leave your shirt on. Without question I fight to get out my too tight jeans.

I am thinking to myself wow I was planning something special for him, but it seems like he has got something up his sleeve also and I am so fucking excited right now. And tight I might add the cream ought to have kicked in by now, back to the matter at hand I do as I told and step out the car putting my heals back on as I exit Sebastian is right there to hold my hands we walk to the front of the car where he leans me up on the hood, he kisses me and says sit up and lay back Mya as I did he grab my legs and put them up on the hood. I hear him say look up at the stars Mya and relax we have all night. Open your legs baby and slide down just a little; I did as I am told, Sebastian started laughing I said what is wrong with you.

He said Mya don't get mad at me ok? As he continued laughing I was thinking like his drunk ass is tripping right now. What Sebastian I said. he said ok Mya promise you won't get mad I said ok wearily. Did you wash your ass before you came to the bar? What the fuck kind of question is that what the fuck do I stink or something? No Mya once again calm the fuck down I was just asking because of what I am going to be doing to you. Well fuck it I am not in the fucking mood I shouted get the fuck off me I went home and showered and got dress you fucking asshole I feel humiliated right now.

As the tears stroll down my eyes I instantly feel bad that I called him an asshole the look of shock in his eyes Sebastian pulled me to him and said calm down Mya I was just joking with you please don't cry. Holding me close Sebastian planted soft kisses on my face kissing away my tears. Now why the fuck he insulted me, and I end up being the one feeling like shit damn.

Soft kisses on my neck is making me relax again we are standing by the passenger side door my back is toward the car I can feel his hands caressing my back, he reaches up to

184

kiss my lips and we kiss passionately I am saying sorry and so is he the passion began to brew the buttons on my shirt are being popped off Sebastian make circles with his tongue around my nipples one at time he slides down to his knees licking my inner thighs blowing on my swollen clit he said watch me baby don't take your eyes off me. In a soft voice I said ok he sunk his head between my legs and began his brutal tongue whipping the cool air and the warmth of his tongue felt like heaven. Slowly and softly I look down at him and he is making love to me with underneath the stars I am so fucking hot for you right now I cried. I want to hear you Mya there is no one out here moan as loud as you like baby. I arch my back a little and leaned my head back and look up at the stars and moaned as loud as I could I called out his name Sebastian oh baby right there baby yes it feels so good daddy why you are doing me like this my moans turned into heavy panting I can feel my body tighten I am about to explode I pant don't stop daddy I am about to cum Sebastian stopped I cried out loud nooooooo please nooo baby don't stop. Not yet Mya relax we got all night let the air cool you down a little I promise it will be worth the wait. I don't want to lose the mood so I hide my disappointment and go with the flow come over here baby he motioned I got back on the hood this time I spread my legs and slide down as he got on his knees I put one hand on his head and pull him in I grind my hot wet pussy in his lips I raised my head a little and look between my legs Sebastian eyes are close and he is licking and sucking with passion I am trying to enjoy it longer but the sight of his tongue punishing my clit is making my legs shake oh baby I pant, you got me so too hot I am about to fucking combust I screamed Sebastian in a high pitch voice I swear it echoed. That familiar tightening feeling in my pelvic was intense I feel like heat is coming out of me, my clit is hard I pull his head in and grind my clit to the motion of his tongue. Stick out your tongue let me see it lick my clit baby! OH, fuck yeah like that Sebastian just like that, my legs gave way and I exploded screaming and screaming my body is shaking tears are running down my eyes wow that was one of the best orgasms I've ever had I said as if I lost my voice and could not speak.

Oh Mya come here baby let me hold you I know how much you love to please me I wanted to return goodness to you I love baby I want to be able to satisfy you just as much as you satisfy me and let me clear the air because I don't want to go home with any tension I was just joking with you Mya at the time I just thought it was funny I know that you go through great lengths to keep yourself clean for me and I admire that about you so forgive me please Mrs. Gutierrez. You are all forgiven my love and I am sorry for overreacting and calling you an asshole that is not what I think of you at all I am truly sorry baby I replied. Let us let it go Mya it was all a misunderstanding and we are all good now let's go home and fuck unless you want it right here under the stars all you gotta do is bend over and touch your toes okay I am game I said Sebastian looked surprise I said I want to get this all out while I can and nobody can hear us it feel good to call your name out loud so let's just fuck out here right now you got me leaking yep soaking wet and here comes the song I like this one so I let it play in my head I wish I could think of a song and from my thoughts it plays on the radio that would be awesome I could drop it while its hot right now.

Turning around I spread on the hood and spread my legs wide but something sexier came on the radio late night jam Crown Royal on Ice by Jill Scott live at the House of Blues oh yeah its going down I feel Sebastian slide in the electricity flows through my body, his hard dick slide in and out of me in a rhythmic way that had me so fucking aroused. I screamed his name as I came I can feel his hands sliding up my back as I tilt my head back he grabs my neck I climbed up on the hood ass up face down Sebastian growls in a deep voice damn baby your pussy tight like a glove on my dick right now, open it up lemme see it shit slide down a little mama! This feels so fucking good right now babe ooh feels like the first time.

Spread them legs a little sexy! I do as I am told but oh fuck I am about to buss at the sound of voice it feels crazy out here the wind slightly blowing and here we go daddy starts his punishment I'm giving it back to him looking up at the stars in a sexy voice I cried oh fuck me daddy Sebastian groan and said say it again Mya in a deep by this time my pussy about to either collapse in ecstasy or give up the pome ghost I can feel the fire inside burning I am about to fucking explode I screamed fuck daddy you going make me cum all over your rock hard dick, I can fuck you all the time come on by Jerimiah ooh, ooh ,ooh is all I can say my juices are flowing my muscles are tense my breathing is heavy I feel Sebastian fingers touch my clit which is at attention oh baby I pant you know exactly what to do.

Grinding my clit to his fingers and feeling his hard- thrust inside of me I screamed take your pussy baby Sebastian slammed into me I screamed again fuck your pussy daddy it's all yours. Fuck Mya he growled I am going to cum inside you stay still bitch don't move. I bust out laughing yeah whatever dude hurry up my knees are killing me. Then stay still bitch I ain't gonna say it again you just prolonging the climax Mya baby! Hmm I think to myself bitch you better pull the freak card and get this shit over with. I blurt out to Sebastian you know I am your little slut fuck me like you just paid me daddy, before he could respond I said come on daddy your dick is the best I ever fucked so bust this pussy open my panting get louder and louder, tightening and releasing my pelvic muscles I can feel him jump inside oh yeah he is about to buss his fingers are working magic on my clit I am about to pass the fuck out on his dick plus my knee caps are about to give out.

Sebastian screamed out my name as he slammed into me his voice got deeper all I can hear was I am about to cum in this hot pussy baby I replied come for me daddy as I said that I could feel my release coming and his I screamed at the top of my voice I am coming baby. Sebastian replied oh fuck yeah Mya let me feel that wetness oh yeah baby I am about to buss I can hear him, and I can feel the swelling of his dick inside of me as he releases he screams I love you baby oh fuck Yeah, I love you Mya. And the tears started to run down my eyes so much emotions and feelings all at once he laid on top of me as he climaxed I can feel soft kisses on my neck, but I can't hide my emotions I want to turn around I want to hold him, but he has me pinned down when he realized I was crying he immediately got up and turned me around his hands on my face he looks confuse what's wrong Mya? He asked I said baby this is the second time you made me cry tonight the way you take hold of my body it's a feeling I just can't explain and just hearing you say that you love me just made me feel warm inside I know that I will be content with you for the rest of my life the way I feel when you are inside of me the connection and the intense feeling sometimes I think that I would pass out it's like fire and more fire and I need your water hose to put out it that's the only way I can explain it.

Yeah but sometimes Mya I don't know if I am really satisfying you! Wait before you get upset let me explain. Sebastian, I don't want to hear it I respond as I wave my hands and turn my face away, really you do satisfy me if you did not I would not be around I am always eager to be in your arms Sebastian I don't want you to feel that way.

Sexy 12

Mya shut up for a minute and allow me to explain myself I can express my own feelings very well listen baby I love to satisfy you too. Sebastian said as his eyes welled up so did mines and here comes to water works because it breaks my heart to see him cry.

He continues Mya your sex drive is off the fucking radar and I just try to keep up with you the best I can and shhh, don't speak he motions as he places one finger on my lips I know that my world would come apart if I don't have you by my side the chemistry between us is crazy I feel the electricity to and man I can't even begin to explain it but I know it out of the atmosphere the way I feel when I am deep inside of you I guess what I am trying to say is that I just want to take you there like you take me I want you to feel as satisfied as you satisfy me I want you Mya. He leans in and kiss me and whispers, but my ass is getting cold out here let's go home I will run us a hot bath and we can cuddle and maybe if your lil ass behave yourself you might get some hot chocolate with whip cream on the top.

Umm yummy I replied hmm I will have to try to be a good little girl! Now stop all that crying if I did not know better I would think that your lil ass is pregnant with all them damn emotions you keep having we might just have to get you tested I know you got one of those tests stashed somewhere, I giggled how do you know what I got stashed mister? Don't worry about all that Mya come on love lets go home now that extra order of wings is calling my name baby. We going to fight for them wings because right now I am famished to bad that sports bar don't have driven through.

You know Mya I can have the bartender number I can call him and order more wings and have him bring it out when we get there but we will have to tip him. Sebastian, I don't have a problem with tipping him IF we don't have to come out of the car is all I care about let me I have some cash so call him I want an order of the garlic wings though.

Ok babe let me call him you drive that way when we pull up he can be on my side I don't need anybody seeing your freshly fucked ass right now. Ha you got jokes whatever if you wanted me to drive just say I know I wore you out homey so it's all good. Mya please you wore me out? Let me ask you this who the fuck was crying about their knees and shit? I think it was your ass the way I had them legs trembling I was almost starting to feel sorry for you! he mocked. Shut the hell up no you didn't say that Sebastian! I laughed. Ah huh Mya let call the bartender and place our orders by the time we got to the restaurant the wings were ready he tipped the bartender forty dollars I just looked like what the hell all he did was walk his ass from behind the bar I said them some expensive wings baller! Don't fucking start Mya he through in a bottle of Patron Silver so we don't have to stop at the liquor store smart ass.

Ah ok Mr. Gutierrez thank you for your explanation of things you don't have to act like that. Mya please let's go home baby before you get fucked for being a smart ass in this parking lot and to tell the truth I would not give a flying seven-forty-seven fuck who saw us fucking. Shit in that case solider let me get out this parking lot before you start your assault "NAS" I turned up the radio to calm the mood Jon B "Tu Amor" comes on the radio Sebastian hands slides around my neck and he begins to sing, I love it I smiled all the way home this is what love feels like the beautiful moments like right now even my conscious is happy that hefer, ain't saying a word. We pulled in and it feels good to be home I am happy that there is no work tomorrow, so I can sleep in as late as I want to. Sebastian get the bags as I open the door for us to get in I hit the alarm on the car and we are in home sweet home.

Mya go run our bath and I will prepare our food! Ok babe I responded I quickly wipe down the tub, hmm where is the bath salt that he loves let me see I am going to make this sexy I think I have some rose petals in the refrigerator ok I've manage to wipe down the tub, turning the water on I quickly run to the kitchen and get the rose petals out I look and baby is getting the table ready for us to eat smiling to myself I think I love when we get along and things are going beautiful this is love I will say it over and over and again.

Hey sexy? Sebastian look over I said you look so fucking sexy right now baby after our bath I will lick you, dry baby. Don't fucking start that shit Mya! What hold up even when I am being nice you scolding, me babe why you got to act like this. He laughed and said I am sorry baby I am tripping, you got the water running?

I said yes daddy and walk away. The music comes on and all I can here is I can fuck you all the time Jeremih, oh shit it ain't over I come outside baby gives me a shot of Patron and let's get in the water this song is the damn shit the beat is crazy.

Sebastian said hold up baby let's eat something first I am famished from earlier today come over here and sit down for a minute pretty baby. Ok honey I replied let me check on the tub I will turn the water off that way we don't flood the neighbors okay? Yeah ok Mya hurry the fuck up please baby I want you here with me I know you doing something for us but I miss your touch already. OH, shit I have got to hurry the fuck up this is the Sebastian I love the man that needs me next to him that makes me feel so important my fiancé, my soon to be husband right about now he has no clue that he just sealed the envelope for us. I know now better than I've known before that this man is truly all of mines no more searching I have found him wow I am twisted right now I let the music play.

I feel content and relaxed I look up sand our eyes are locked into each other Sebastian winks his eyes at me I smile crimson damn I am such a sucker for this man I almost can't help myself I don't have a care in this world at this moment just pure bliss or whatever you call it all I know is that life is good and I am not looking back moving forward is the way to go. The mood is so right the food was excellent and most of all the dick is good I can't help but smile as the thoughts cross my mind because the feeling goes right to my inner thighs my clit is like a dick it gets so fucking aroused it's almost like this fucking pussy have a mind of her own I just can't control this bitch I do wonder about being faithful sometimes if I can let Gisele get down hmm even the thought of her tongue makes me want to scream my conscious Y'all at me like really bitch do we need to have this conversation right now you are going to ruin the blasted moment what the fuck is wrong with you.

I hear Sebastian voice saying earth to Mya I look up and he is standing right in front of me stoking my face I smiled. Is everything okay he asked quickly I snapped out of it and resume my prior deposition still thinking damn the rest of my life with this man I sure hope I am ready. Come on honey focus my conscious warns I am getting a little tired I sigh let's get in the tub babes bring the bottle of Patron and once again it's on like popcorn baby. Mya, you think your ass would have had enough that damn pussy should be warn the fuck out by now says Sebastian. But any way let's eat first the food is ready I don't want to have a hangover in the morning and I sure ain't trying to pick your ass up from the floor so let's eat now. I sigh okay baby you right I am little hungry so that will work then we can chill out. I sashay across the room to the dining table Sebastian pulled my chair the food is still, warm so we eat in silence occasionally we glance at each other and smile the sparkle in his eyes tells it all I know he loves my hot pussy ass and I love him too without a doubt these damn wings are so good right now I take another shot of Patron and winked my eyes at Sebastian hurry up slow poke I mock him we got some hot water waiting on us. Slow down Mya what is the big rush you got something up your sleeves or what. Not exactly Mr. I am warned out and I want to slip in the hot water and relax so come the fuck on slow poke and stop asking me all them damn questions before I leave your ass out here alone. As I completed my sentence, I took off running when I saw Sebastian push his chair; him and the expression on his face says oh you done it now.

Don't run bitch Sebastian screams you want to talk shit stand your ass right and deal with the repercussions. Running and screaming, I try to lock the bedroom door but to no avail on quick instinct I ran to the bathroom door as I took one step and I can feel Sebastian arms around me and I am off my feet I giggle like a little school girl one slap on my ass and I can feel the sting I holla damn Sebastian your heavy hand ass what the fuck you trying then out of the blue he stopped and asked so did anything ever happen with you and Gisele?

I looked baffled shaking my head I said what why are you asking me that question in the middle of us having a great time are you, serious right now I said pretending to be angry but deep down I am scared shitless my heart is racing I keep telling myself to keep a straight face my conscious is smirking like yeah let me see your ass get out of this shit. Sebastian looked at me and what the fuck was that a trick question answer- me. I immediately responded NO any more questions? Why the hell are you so upset Mya I am just asking a question?

Sebastian right now at this moment when we had a wonderful evening really? Why did you ask me that, answer me? Mya it's just been bothering me and since you dream I can't help but wonder. OH, my Gosh why are you rehashing old shit was I talking in my sleep or something.

No Mya calm the fuck down you are making me think something did happen from the way that you are acting now you know we are getting married don't make me think twice about giving you this ring if you are not honest with me right now I know you and I got a hunch that something went down now get it off your chest now because this is your free pass. I looked at him and something inside my conscious was like bitch you better shut the fuck up this is the perfect definition of a set up. I said NO and stomped off now I'm fucking pist off like don't fucking threaten me if you are having second thoughts just say so I yelled as I slam the bathroom door I immediately locked it and slid down the door to the floor with my hand to my mouth like oh shit.

You are looking guilty right now even though I am wrong and strong I won't fucking give in this is not the time he practically ruin, our whole night. I hear a knock on the door I screamed go the fuck away Sebastian and leave me the fuck alone. Talk to me Mya I don't want to talk if you want to threaten me maybe there is something you are hiding so let me make this shit a little easier for you the engagement is off so keep the fucking ring. Sebastian yells open the door and bangs on the door got louder open the fucking door Mya before I break this shit down and you know that I will. No go away I don't want to talk to you, you manage to ruin our night there are no words to describe how I feel right now. Just let me take my shower in peace please. I manage to get my ass from the cold ass floor.

I slide in the tub rocking back and forth my chin in my knees my arms wrapped my legs I am so scared OMG really is this happening to us right now why right now my head is about to bust wide open my heart is about to bust out of my chest fuck I can't breathe maybe I should tell him and get it over with instead of carrying this weight on my back I did not do her she did me hell so technically I did not cheat. I got in and out the tub quickly because my head is spinning I feel faint suddenly, the tears started to roll and I cannot stop these tears I know that I am wrong walking to the door I open it an laid on the bed sobbing Sebastian is gone and I feel dumber than a box of rocks. I quickly call his cell phone baby please come home I plead. Please, where are you?

Sebastian replies I am away from you and that's what I really want right now there is something going on and if you don't speak up you will lose me and I fucking mean it Mya you are currently pissing me the fuck off so speak up now. Sebastian screamed! OH, shit he is really fired up but you know what, in my mind I really want to be an ass right now and cuss this muther fucker out for yelling and being so fucking demanding but shit I am in the wrong, so I have to take this one. Ah I feel like running into a hole right now and hiding. Mya answer me now! Sebastian screams in a stern voice. Okay I yelled shit come home and we will talk I am not having this conversation over the phone seriously Sebastian I said with my voice cracked. Please?

I whimper. He said yeah ok I will be ther,e and I thought to myself with a smile across my face yes, I love winning even though it's not over yet my conscious is like you conniving ass bitch! Fall back bitch I quickly demanded moving on quickly thinking out loud Hmm let me see I've got to find something loose and comfortable no panties or bra though I've got to work this one without seeming like I am trying too hard. Rushing to gather myself I hear the door open and my heart just about jumped out of my chest and was heading for the nearest exit quickly I slipped on my night gown, put a little Vaseline on my lips and walk out to the living room where Sebastian was fixing us a glass of Hennessy yep it's about to be serious up in here.

I take a deep breath and walk towards him almost exasperated at this point in the back of my mind I am saying shit I ain't got time for this fucking shit seriously. Here we go Hi baby I mutter he looks at me and rolled his eyes. Now

I am thinking let us pray because he is about to annoy the living daylights out of me with his fucked up- attitude. This is going to be easy at first ,I was nervous now I am like I don't give a flying seven forty-seven fuck. That saying taken from my favorite rapper NAS! I said Sebastian don't be like that as I tilt my head to the side he looked at me with them don't fuck with me eyes and I just spilled the juice.

Like a damn dumb bitch, with his hand rubbing his face Sebastian shook his head and laugh Mya I don't know what the fuck to do with your ass seriously you trip me out. Look I am tired, and I want to go to bed Mya I am going to take a shower good night.

Ok baby that's fine with me I said feeling a sign of relief I make us some tea so by the time he gets out the shower he can relax a little I am going must put in work, so I better squeeze some lemon in my tea because by the time I get done sucking his dick my throat would need some lemon love. And I know he is going to hold back on purpose.

Sebastian gets out the shower I said here is some tea babe, he nods hmm okay this is going to be a little more, harder. I strip and put on my red bottoms heals I get the massage oil and I looked at him with these please baby let me make it up to you with pleading eyes but in the back of my mind I'm like don't fuck around and get cussed out shit I'm trying here. Sebastian looks at me with a smirk on his face he already know, what it is and he is willing to let me look like an ass because I am guilty of the crime. He sat up in the bed drinking his tea I straddle him and slide down, so my ass is in the air and my head is down getting ready to get it poppin, on his ass.

What are you up to Mya? I smirked and slid down towards his feet pour some oil on his legs and commence to doing my magic with my figures well actually I'm mimicking the lady in the nail shop either way my aim is to please. Massaging both legs I work my way up sliding my hand up and down that curved wood with oil.

Sexy 13

Sebastian moans and I can feel the warmth between my legs. Moving pass, it I straddle him place some oil in my hands rubbing his shoulders and his chest down I'm looking in his eyes I scoot up on him grinding slowly I whisper lean up a little honey so I can rub your back my breasts are all over his chest I can feel Sebastian hands slowly coming up my back I dig my fingers into his back and grind there is enough oil on his body to lubricate mine I made sure of it.

I lick his neck the moans a growing louder my cunt is wet as fuck I'm about to cum all over your dick I whispered to Sebastian. Damn Mya talk nasty to me baby I love it when you do that shit be my lil freak mama. Oh, Daddy grab my ass my pussy is about to explode on your hard dick. My panting gets louder and louder, I can feel the heat my body is building up I'm about to cum I grind harder on Sebastian calling out his name as I unravel over him my body trembles and with one quick move Sebastian slides his dick inside of me and I love it my body is wrapped around him and I am taking every inch of his loins.

In one swift turn he pushes me to the edge of the bed and stands up my legs wrapped around his legs and I can feel every inch I cry out it threw me over my legs started shaking I feel warm pure ecstasy Sebastian slaps my ass I scream out loud the trust and the slap made me cum. Oh Daddy I pant fuck me harder Sebastian moaned, oh fuck yeah Mya talk all that shit I want to hear it, tell me baby what you what me to do to you.

I responded I really want you to pull out and eat my pussy but your dick so bomb I'm about to explode all over it right now when I think about the way this man turns me on its un real my body craves his touch my panting gets heavier as I tighten my muscles between my legs explode all over his Grade A Type Premium Dick damn my juices are flowing I can feel every inch of him inside hit that baby I scream fuck it just beat it up Daddy it's all I tighten by doing Kegel exercises which is making me so freaking moist I'm working my hot wet pussy all over his dick I'm panting he is biting me on my neck and I'm loving it I cannot get enough of this man my body craves him when he is not around his scent entices me I want him all of him deep inside of me so I grind harder and harder letting him all in letting him fill me up his jabs are short and stiff. I want to cum Daddy I scream he slapped my ass and without hesitation I came all in full force I screamed and came at the same time squirting all over Sebastian I love you baby I whimper he was like yeah now gimme that ass that's what I want tonight, Oh fuck! Watch your mouth Mya and yeah that's what's about to happen to your ass right now so come yeah let me punish the pussy good with my tongue and lick that ass like you like it come sit on my face.

Mama I quickly sit on his face it seems like my pussy flew in his mouth before I could actually move my body it feel so amazing the his tongue as it caresses my clit oh yeah its fucking awesome dude I can cry but fuck I really want to pass out my legs are shaking and the tongue play is ferocious damn daddy I ain't gonna last Is that right Mya, cause I need you to cum twice before your punishment be making a bitch want to spend all her money on you and your mama. he stops looks up at me and smile shaking his head he said your ass is crazy Mya and I love it I'm about to put on the big girl panties and let him hit this ass the way he wants it. but really- inside I'm about to scream out loud its good once it's in but the initial contact is brutal shit ky jelly please.

I whisper he said I got this passenger driver, I run this shit as he said hit I felt hot spit hit my ass oh fuck no you did not in a dark sexy voice Sebastian said, oh fuck yeah I did with that I felt a jab oh fuck you Sebastian hell no slow the fuck down May if you keep talking shit Ima go fuck you in the cold pool downstairs scream at that! YES, honey I quickly replied in a pleading voice because I know this Mutha fucker will pick my ass and haul me downstairs and fuck me in the second hit he was gently with a stifle laugh he says see when you behave how easy this is?

I really want to reply what the fuck ever but shit I ain't in the mood for cold water plus a dick in my ass the thought of it sends chills down my spine giving me the ibby jibbies. in the back of my mind Gisele is present oh shit not now but wait when I think of her pretty ass eating my pussy the juices flow them pretty eyes she is so beautiful I'm about to cum jiz oh Sebastian! OH, shit did I just call her name?

Bitch you know what you said with your careless ass my conscious screams you dumb as a box of rocks bitch. Delete your account bitch! I scream to my conscious. fuck he is hitting me hard did he hear me my face was in the pillow oh fuck Mya I screamed my conscious was like you, dumb bitch you dumb for fucking real I should leave your ass for real I ain't lying they should give your dumb ass the stupid award... ascribed Mya is a dumb ass, who does this shit? hold on don't respond allow me ah you!

I'm out...ps. your sane conscious. Aww fuck what you heard, and hold told you are my conscious I don't get dismiss I dismiss you bitch don't get life twisted! now back to our regular schedule program. This man hitting like I'm the blasted enemy, but truth be told if the shoe was one the other foot you would be on go mode right now my winner, take this dick because there are no fucking words to express the dumb shit you just blurted out calling Gisele when your man hitting you looking to be the victim in a murder case tonight shit. what the hell am I thinking that right there was a blonde moment.

Sebastian, I screamed oh baby cum for me all I heard was shut the fuck up Mya I don't want to hear a word coming out of your mouth what's wrong baby I whispered oh you know what the fucks wrong Mya I choose to play innocent I was like I don't know what you are talking about baby. Slam I jumped he hitting this fucker going for broke I screamed stop he said what the fuck for you calling a bitch name while we fucking you disrespecting me? MYA, I screamed no you crazy I did not call her name at all are you, serious right now?

Of course, you know I got to make his ass feel like he crazy shit I hope I can pull this shit off or else its war on my body right now. Babe you are tripping right now I said in an exasperated voice like really dude just stop babe please just stop I said stop he howled I was like yes, he said I ain't, cum yet I was like well hurry the fuck up because now you are pissing me off. Slam he hit that shit hard as fuck I jumped off this time he pulled me back flipped me around and went in the pussy, now we face to face I'm searching his face at this point I'm feeling like I can still get away with this shit my eyes are pleading with his like please don't start with me baby I don't want to fight I whisper. I love only you to him and I can see a smile on his lips and I know I've got to cut the shit out and behave at the end of the day I've got to deal with fascination or whatever the fuck it is with Gisele before I lose my man, and my dear that would be ugly.

I need him like the body needs blood. as I relax he climax took you long enough I whispered Sebastian push me off him and said now go wash your wet cunt. I said hey you better watch your mouth or else! Sebastian spin around so fast and got in my face with this mean ass look on his face he said or what Mya? rolling my eyes in the back of my head because I'm not all intimidated by his ass I slide my hand under him and grab his dick and said or else your little big man won't get to slide up in her wet cunt again. shit that's fine with me Sebastian said I'll hit up that nice tight ass from now on I released that dick so fast and screamed oh hell no you have lost your mind boo. Rolling my eyes now come wash me up sexy, nah I'll pass Mya I'm done fucking with you for the day I've had enough I need some me time. Annoyed Mya said fine you want some time you going to get that and walked into the shower slamming the door.

Oh he is really starting to piss me off to the extreme I'm going wash my ass and get dress and get the fuck out of here shit he got to be careful of what he is asking for he just might get it. I'll text my Mom and chill over there for the night and that's that. Sebastian knocks on the door let me in Mya. Hell, no was the response coming from the other side of the door come on Mya stop playing. No Sebastian you stop playing I'll be out in a minute and you can get your me time, Mya you are such a smart ass but alright then hurry up and get out. Oh you have no idea Mya whispered I'm trying to move like the speed of light asshole. You said something Mya I can't hear you? I did not respond because I was not in the mood I'm irritated to the extreme, ok here we go the task of facing him ok calm down Mya take your temperature down don't escalate nothing just quietly leave smh I emerged saying nothing at all Sebastian made smart remark it's about time what took you so long.

I did not reply I just went on about my business the key is to disappear before he comes out of the shower I hear him singing in the shower and suddenly, I feel bad for leaving. But I got to go I can't let him treat me like that; wait bitch you might want to take advantage of his singing and stay I'll go prepare us something to eat because as much as I want to be an ass the status of our relationship is hanging on by thread. I might not want to induce any more labor pains to piss him off, so his T-shirt and no panties you would think after that brutal assault my ass would know better and put some boy shorts on at least. Off to the refrigerator let's see what we must cook. ok we have beef for fajitas, corn tortillas for baby and flour for me. I need bell peppers onion and tomatoes oh the jalapeños I get to cooking I hear me amour singing.

My background bitch rears her ugly head talking about, bitch you better cook that for that sexy man before he leave, your curious ass. shut the fuck up I scowled at her ass so fast. I'm like bitch you are dismissed get the fuck out here, exit stage left bitch. Now back to it cut up my vegetables grill my meat, Daddy comes out the shower he walks into the kitchen slaps me on the ass, and says let me get a shot of tequila bartender. Rolling my eyes, I say I'm the cook the maid and the bartender, I got you bae but you need to be tipping my ass in cash. MYA, I tip your ass in dick that's about it! he laughs. Whatever Sebastian here you go let me pour me one too, we having fajitas babe? Sebastian asks. Yeah you know how I like to be ask obvious questions I just looked at his ass and replied with three letters of the alphabet DUH! Sebastian spins around you know what Mya you keep up that shit you hear me. Hmm ok I quickly respond and take my shot and pour another I'm not in the mood so we gonna keep the temperature down. Yeah Bitch you better I hear in my head followed by shut the fuck up background bitch Arrivederci.

Food is almost done I sliced some avocados set the table now I'm thinking oh shit I did not make any rice. Luckily there is a bag of Spanish rich in the cabinet I put that on quickly. Now for shot two Sebastian looking at me so I pour another since he is being fucking nosey and shit. He looks out of the corner of his eyes and says Mya I'm watching you, shrugging my shoulders I side eye his ass too like what the fuck ever.

Now I have no idea why I'm in between worlds right now I'm trying to be cool, but something is brewing in the background maybe I should have left and taken some time for me instead of pretending shit. Fuck I need a Prozac or something I'm tripping for no apparent reason at all. We sit down to eat and I'm like babe I need some weed or something to calm my nerves. Sebastian fork stops in midair you need what? You heard me I said I need some weed as in Marri Do you Juana.As in Kush as in Snoop you got it now? Yeah, Yeah Mya what's wrong with you? Smh.I thought I just explained that to you like please be present in the room! Oh, yeah you are getting out of control Mya I ain't fucking with you right now so take another shot. And eat your food I'll arrange your smoke for you later, Ok? Thank you I responded thank you babe sorry for being an ass.

With a smirk Sebastian replied you're excused wifey!

Smiling back at, him I'm thinking to myself Bitch you've been warned get it to fuck together please. Phone rings What the fuck is Gisele calling me for? Before I knew it, I said that shit out loud I look at Sebastian the fucking fork in midair again fuck I'm dead. I answer the phone like ah hello how in fuck can I help you? Before she could reply Sebastian says in a stern voice, put that bitch on speaker right fucking now Mya. Like a two year, old who just got in trouble I feel a strong urge to take a shit bitch. Really, I felt this shit coming on since earlier, she responds Hi Mya I'm sorry to disturb you. Yeah you are disturbing me I'm having an intimate dinner with my soon to be husband.

What you want Gisele? I asked in an annoyed voice. But deep down I'm scared as fuck because Sebastian is about to make me give up the ghost. Then this bitch replied; Well since you asked like that Mya I really want to see you, I would like to spend some time with you. Sebastian roars wait a fucking minute this bitch bold as fuck! Give me the phone Mya, I happily pass the phone to him because I need him to unleash that anger exactly where it belongs. Because this inappropriate bitch done went to the store bought the gun, put her name on the bullet and about to pull the trigger herself. All I can say it's better you than me bitch, I'm trying to dodge this line of fire. I feel like Mufasa is in the building Sebastian roar scared the shit out of me shit. You might want to go check your pants my conscious screams why you, dumb bitch I scream.

Then I heard Gisele you have lost your fucking mind disrespecting me, now know that I will fight your ass like a man for my wife. Gisele screams technically she ain't your wife yet Sebastian! What? Sebastian screams bitch I live at 2298 Jamal Street #7 google that and come see what I got for you. Although that sounds enticing Sebastian I'll pass on your dick I want your woman, or should I say soon to be wife? Yo lil bitch where you live at where your mama living at? Sebastian screams hold on wait I know where you work you want to fuck with me dude? Who are you calling dude Gisele screams. You dude Sebastian yells pull up your boxers you like women it is what it is. For future reference you should stay in your lane but since you got in my lane welcome me bitch! You know what Sebastian I'm on the way Gisele screams. Oh, hell nah I screamed nope not to fucking day bitch.

Get the fuck off my phone and don't call back or ever speak to me again. Sebastian screams over me you know the address dude? Which dude seems to be infuriating the fuck out of Gisele she screams see you soon Mya kisses and hung up. Sebastian threw the phone across the room that vein in the middle of his forehead done popped out oh yes, its war. I'm sitting still I can barely breathe lungs don't fail me no, I look over at Sebastian like why did you give her our address but I decided to think it and not say it for obvious reasons. So, I blurted out well fuck let me get dress this female is on the way to our home. No Mya we don't cater to stray bitches stay as you are. OH, fuck my heart is in my throat like a dick in drawers shit why why- whyyyyy I screamed in my head.

My bitch was like shh bitch you are disturbing me, I'm not having this conversation in my head with you itch back off and go scratch yourself in a corner. Fifteen minutes pass I'm about to take another shot of tequila then I hear the phone rig I go to get it it's the front gate Gisele is here Sebastian. So, what Mya buzz that bitch in now what's the matter you scared. See you want to play these games so now we are going to bring everything to light tonight Mya go get your Orville Redenbacher, the movie is about to begin Fuck I'm scared as I turn around I hear her heals coming up the steps. Then the knock on the door.... Oh, shit

217

I'm about to pass the fuck out! Before my legs buckle on me my conscious go in for the kill, all I heard you is a wimp, I couldn't even reply fuck you I just went down fuck I'm out cold its dark in here But, why I can still here my conscious saying dumb bitch!

Part 2 soon!